The
DANGERS
of PROXIMAL
ALPHABETS

The
DANGERS
of PROXIMAL
ALPHABETS

KATHLEEN ALCOTT

OTHER PRESS NEW YORK

Copyright © 2012 Kathleen Alcott
Production Editor: Yvonne E. Cárdenas
Book design: Cassandra J. Pappas
This book was set in 11.75 pt. Garamond MT by
Alpha Design & Composition of Pittsfield, NH.

10 9 8 7 6 5 4 3 2 1

Library of Congress Cataloging-in-Publication Data

Alcott, Kathleen.
  The dangers of proximal alphabets / Kathleen Alcott.
    p. cm.
  ISBN 978-1-59051-529-7 (pbk.) — ISBN 978-1-59051-530-3 (ebook)
1. Brothers and sisters—Fiction.   2. Childhood—Fiction.
3. Art—Fiction.   4. Domestic fiction.   I. Title.
  PS3601.L344D36 2012
  813'.6—dc23

                                                    2011050300

Publisher's Note:
This is a work of fiction. Names, characters, places, and incidents either are the product of the author's imagination or are used fictitiously, and any resemblance to actual persons, living or dead, events, or locales is entirely coincidental.

This book is dedicated with manifold variants of love
to Casey Cripe, a brilliant narrator.

"if there is a place further from me I beg you do not go"
—FRANK O'HARA, "Morning"

The
DANGERS
of PROXIMAL
ALPHABETS

Our parents liked to say that the first time Jackson and I met, we concentrated our focus so intently, grew so still, that they worried our little bodies might have forgotten we'd exited our watery beginnings, neglected the duty to breathe in and out. On the floor of the living room we turned our still-soft skin toward each other and blinked before demonstrating our talents in gripping and releasing: my five fingers around his chubby wrist, then his in embrace of mine. They say that the cat, our relative equal in size but a fascinating stranger in composition, strolled up to sniff the crowns of our heads, our full cheeks, but we offered him no attention. My mother and father and Julia, sitting on the couch, all happy with disbelief at the way their endlessly curious infants had quickly adopted such content with a tiny corner of the universe.

The next part of the story, the one that would echo for decades afterward: Julia moved to scoop Jackson from the floor. I left my quiet behind and howled with such force that the cat, still skirting the carpet, panicked and ran. My mother came to me and attempted comfort; my father, at the door with Julia, shrugged and offered a comment about the volatile nature of young love. They laughed, of course, and agreed to bring us together again very soon. Jackson did not cry, but squirmed from Julia's restraint and tried to get a clearer vision of me. My wailing gained confidence and rhythm. I refused, even, the draw of my mother's breast, as if I knew that she would not be my family much longer, that I would find that elsewhere.

That night my parents broke their oath to leave me in the crib, no matter how upset, and brought me into their bed. They wondered at me where I lay between them, linked their fingers over the heaving abdomen they'd created together, sang me folk songs about low roads and high roads, told me the word for each part of my body, whispered secrets about the ocean and the brain and the patterns of the earth until I finally calmed enough to listen.

Jackson has one green eye and one brown, though each is dotted with bits of the other color, as if hesitant to vehemently commit. He has a mole on his left hip (noncancerous, last time he checked) and half a BB bullet permanently lodged in his right shoulder blade (I put it there). His cheeks are wide and globular, as if they were hiding apples for later consumption, and give him the appearance of someone instantly trustworthy and kind. He is uncircumcised, but his foreskin is unusually taut and so this isn't obvious. The hair on his chest issues forth in small tight curls, and halfway across the spirals change their direction. He pronounces "often" with a harsh "t." When he picks up the phone he goes, "'Lo?!" in mock surprise to be hearing a voice from the magic box in his hand. He is a master with chopsticks. He is endlessly polite to the men at corner stores, taxi drivers, weary all-night-diner waitresses. He once dove into the polluted river in our hometown to retrieve a necklace of my mother's after the well-used clasp broke, and contracted a rash that lasted two weeks (he wasn't embarrassed). He talks in his sleep, among other things. He has a tattoo of my name on his chest that he insisted on during the throes of a melo-dramatic fugue (which is rare for his character) when we were seventeen. A mutual friend in a motel room (where his brother James worked the front desk) administered the ink at four a.m. with a questionable needle. He is in-credibly gifted with children, though he always refused to discuss the possibility of having any. He is left-handed and secretly proud of the fact, the implication of genius. He once rode a shopping cart down one of the steepest hills in our city just for the hell of it; in addition to the half BB pellet, there is a bit of gravel, resulting from the inevitable crash at the bottom, that is also permanently part of his body. He is not traditionally handsome but most are tricked into thinking so. There are many items of clothing he has owned for more than ten years and still wears. His second toe is longer than his big toe. He goes through phases of intense love, then hatred for In-dian food (it gives him explosive diarrhea). He is endear-ingly cranky in the mornings but inherently an early riser, and he gives up coffee every six months, swearing this time it's for good. He likes to wear a mustache, but only when accompanied by a beard. If you go to a museum with him, he will unfailingly wander off by himself. He is a talented drinker but rarely seems drunk. He is a library of facts about the ocean. His body temperature is always one to two degrees higher than the average 98.6 and so sleeping with him feels like being in an intimate position with a furnace. He has a way of narrowing his eyes when he is annoyed or suspicious, and a way of ridiculing someone without their noticing until it's too late. He absolutely spurns astrology; his handwriting has a way of changing to suit the occasion. He can roll his *r*'s quite well and, if he chooses to, speaks pretty decent Spanish. He whistles while he urinates. He always carries a knife and uses it (in handy versus violent ways) every chance he gets.

He cries infrequently, and when he does it is silent with a great deal of shoulder shaking. He does his best thinking in the ten minutes after a visit to a planetarium. He can curl his tongue into a U and also a "clover," and is a talented eyebrow raiser. There is a spot with a half-inch circumference below his left jaw where hair does not grow; he has bizarre theories about why. Most of the time he has illicit fireworks purchased in Chinatown on his person. He adores Burnese mountain dogs and lights up at a sighting of one.

I use the present tense here, but it is possible that Jackson actually has given up coffee, that he has covered the tattoo of my name with something else, that he cries openly in front of this new woman. It has been a year, two months, and six days since we spoke. It has been four months since, in a moment of loneliness that came not late at night but early on a sunny morning, I called him and left a message he didn't return. The last of his belongings and mementos of Us sit in a box in the back of my bedroom closet; though I resist the urge to take it down and finger the black-and-white photo booth strips, the silly tin science-fiction lunch box I bought him that he loved fiercely, the only remaining piece of art he made in his sleep, I know the objects so well that I'm not sure what difference it actually makes.

Officially, I'm Ida, though Jackson has called me *I* as long as I can remember. The symbolism is sickening. Even in the worst of it, even in phases where I spoke almost exclusively in monosyllables and guttural sounds and sat around lost in the worn flannel shirt he left behind, I would never bring this up to anyone: *and he calls me* I. *Like* I. *As in* myself.

In a particularly memorable home video, shot by my father who poured his monomania exclusively into filmic evidence of our childhood for a full year before quitting pretty much entirely, Jackson and I are sitting in a sun-faded kiddie pool in my front yard, aged three and a half or four. There's something in my hands Jackson wants but can't have—the camera zooms and focuses—it's a set of brightly colored rubber rings—and he looks right at the camera, at my father, at justice, and cries: *I want it but* I *has it!*

Cut to: Valentine's Day. We are at the kitchen table, our fingers covered in glue and the filth it's attracted, and my father has not taken pains to maintain any level of organization so that bow-tie pasta and bits of stained doily and construction paper and crayons are everywhere. Somewhere in the background you can hear Julia walking a rambunctious James around the house; she is singing "Baby Beluga" full force and he wholeheartedly despite not knowing all the words; my father tries to point the camera toward the sound but it can't be framed and he switches it back to us.

"What," he says, "is Valentine's Day for?"

I ham for the camera and flirt and wiggle: "Loooove," I say.

"And who do you love, honey," says my father, but before I can reply Jackson butts in, his sticky fingers spread wide, grabs my face and plants that series of wet kisses only young children can, and I shriek and giggle.

"I love I!" yells Jackson. "I LOVE I."

Cut to: a celebration ceremony at our kindergarten (the last substantial bit of video for a number of years). We have of course convinced the teachers to let us stand next to each other during the part of the "performance" where the class gets up to sing the alphabet. To his credit, my father covers all four rows of children, with the same historian penchant for accuracy and entirety I've inherited, before settling on the two of us. The many weak voices lilt and strain, and when it gets to "f," you can see our faces widen and bodies tense.

"E, f, g"—Jackson and I look at each other—"h," and then we positively explode as we scream our initials—"I J"—so much so that neither of us has energy for "k"; we've been holding our breath in our ambitious bodies for those two syllables the whole time, and we both sort of slump and stumble, and the shy boy in the tie next to us frowns at how we're embarrassing him.

The majority of our lives we were an exhausting display that others looked on, confused and ashamed to be watching. *I*, at least, was happy to bear witness. But even one letter changes a meaning entirely; no matter their proximity, different points of an alphabet refuse to be represented as the same: there's no guarantee that someone standing at precisely the same longitude and latitude as you will remember the view the same way, no promise that one person's memory of a moment or a month will parallel yours, retain the same value, shape the years of living that follow.

The walls of James and Jackson's bedroom were covered with butcher paper that came in reams wider than it was tall. The paper was spliced together with the Scotch tape their mother kept in the drawer under the telephone, which also held a few photos not worthy of a place on the wall or even the refrigerator, and their father's hammer, which every day acquired rust while we fought off robbers and sunsets.

The sun's obstinate warmth lingered in the asphalt and sidewalk long into the evening while we dreamed. The sun came in through the window every morning at six thirty and offered life to the opposite wall, which displayed an incomplete and frenzied rendering of a circus. In the morning gregarious with childish enthusiasm, the paper circus shifted into a human drama; with the late-afternoon light, the characters became more determined to speak and live intricate, shadowed lives.

That summer, James and Jackson ate their dinners with admirable speed, stamina, and a teeth-baring spirit of anti-

cipated adventure. The forkfuls were violently shoved between their two rows of teeth, and the boys took marked
pleasure in the scraping noise the utensils produced. They
paused, generally in harmony, only at thirty-second inter-
vals, to gulp down bright-colored juice out of bright-colored
cups that their mother set out for them. Sometimes dinner
was followed by a ride on their bright-colored bicycles, but
mostly, just as fiercely as it began, the meal would end—
Jackson's fork would drop, then James's, and the brothers
would look up, expectant, to where their mother sat. Her
consent was generally wordless: a quiet smile or a flick of
hands upward that meant *Go*.

Jackson designated the five to ten minutes after dinner
as a period for solemn thought to be followed by discussion. Jackson, at eight, knew himself to be older, wiser, and
the obvious leader of a project that would surely outlast
them. Despite any planning efforts on the part of his older
brother, James almost always deviated from the strategy.
Jackson understood space and logic, but were it not for
James, the pumpkin-orange tiger on the tight wire would
never have tottered there haphazardly. The circus per-
formers would never have varied ghastly and comically in
height and girth.

Several times their mother put the circus project on hold
and the tiger stood still, the half magicians gruesome beneath the trapeze. Julia suffered migraines that twisted and
writhed in her head, and she often became agitated by the
arguing that swelled in volume from the boys' bedroom.
The source of the tension was, without fail, a matter of cre-
ative differences (e.g., Jackson did not find the oversized

tiger on the tightrope as believable or triumphant as the crown on the top of its head declared it to be). Upon Jackson's expression of disdain for James's artistic endeavors, the younger brother would defend himself violently. There were, he insisted, many reasons for a tiger king.

While we absorbed the paradise of indoor imaginations many afternoons, we valued the wide expanse of our block as well; out there was a wildness the three of us found and cultivated. Overgrown blackberry bushes reached to us through other people's fences, and even after our lips and teeth and tongues were stained purple, the smell lingered and called to us at night while we tossed and turned in the slow heat, while we dreamed of vengeance in the water balloon fights of tomorrow. The brothers had both inherited their father's penchant for sleep talking. Like their father, they spoke not in the stumbling tongues of so many sleep talkers but in full words and careful syllables, giving reason and rhyme to fantastical worlds and images. Unlike their father, though, Jackson and James had partners in their sleep talk. Only myself, the tiger king, the three-quarters-finished clown with crooked purple arms, and the beta fish, who swam the same circles in the same tank (which was situated exactly between the brothers' beds on an end table), were aware of the conversations that took place in the middle of the night, threading strings between the dreamworlds of the brothers. I shared the secret with them, slept with my head almost directly beneath the fish tank, often still in my bright blue bathing suit, with my dark red widow's peak connected, by another invisible thread, to the tip of Jackson's nose.

During the day, I made up for my sex and too-thin stature with calluses thicker than all of the boys'. The balls of my feet were agile and quick; they responded effortlessly to impossibly sharp-angled turns in games of tag and never complained of the heat or the oak roots that reached up through the sidewalk of Madrone Street to remind us of beginnings. I made up for my sex with curse words my father had not meant to teach me, but at night I kept watch of Jackson's chest, monitoring its homogenized ups and downs; the first part of loving anyone is to make sure they're breathing. And so it went that I was the first to witness Jackson and James speaking to each other in the semaphores of deep sleep. Their mother had not noticed; Julia didn't notice a lot of things.

On the last evening of June in that particular circus summer, I sat at the head of Jackson's bed, my legs crossed like a brave Indian warrior, counting his breaths, waiting for an anomaly, sometimes daring to run my index finger over the slight curve of his lips.

Jackson slept like a content old man then, with a slight smile on his face, as if remembering a few sweet picnics and two well-raised children, but I was always scared of him waking. I almost jumped the first time he spoke, before realizing everything was the same.

"In the blond one, where seas go," Jackson said.

My position as guardsman was not found out. The fish still swam their circles, discussing bubbles and miniature

ceramic castles; James, on the other bed, still lay with one
bootied foot outside the covers, but thirty seconds later he
began to speak.

"Dragon time . . . is your time," said some secret part
of James.

And Jackson, after three to five moments: "Sea time?"

And James, whose sleeping head now faced his brother's
bed:

"Yesbutwith the   trains."

". . . with the trains

and the fish man."

" but the fishandthe bridge,

and the . . ."

"Ghost radio!" exclaimed James, and *that* was *that*.

I barely got to sleep that night, twisting and turning
under the odd-smelling guest blanket, trying to make sense
of the strange conversation I'd just witnessed. Ghosts: I
knew plenty about those, having made a lifelong practice
of reaching for my mother, standing in the room where she
took her last breaths and whispering benign details about
my day into the coffee cup my father said was her favorite.
And then, with my father's gift of walkie-talkies the prior
Christmas, into those. There was the radio part, but it had
never occurred to me that the link might exist underwater
until I heard the disembodied words that floated across the
boys' bedroom. A bridge, of course. Of course you'd have
to reach a bridge to get there. To get to her.

M y father's scissors were rusted and unwieldy, heavy like useful things just aren't anymore, and carved shakily into the left blade was the word COPYBOY.

He was born to the editor of a small town's newspaper in the South in 1941 and began writing for the *Courier* as a freshman in high school. When he was sixteen, he was caught skinny-dipping in the community pool, and his punishment was to write the article detailing the event in the crime log. He was unmerciful; he used the word "lascivious"; his father, the editor, was proud.

My father met my mother at the *San Francisco Chronicle*, where she began freelancing and eventually established herself as a fixture. She was tall and everything about her was long; the vertical-striped black-and-white pants she wore frequently that spring further contributed to the impression of a woman who went on forever in every direction. This hint of forever, not just in the length of limbs but also in other dimensions, was probably what initially attracted him. He had hit forty without realizing it: instead of measuring by years, he'd counted his life by the love affairs he'd had in Europe, the red convertible he'd wrapped around an olive tree in Spain, the antiwar riots on college campuses that he'd been lucky enough to witness and report on, the year he'd spent in Hawaii and the volcano he'd watched erupting from his window. Whether there was panic inside him before he met her, or it was meeting her that spawned it, he knew my mother was to be his last conquest; he was confident she was enough to witness for the rest of his life.

She didn't give in at first. She had met many men with bright smiles who tried to equalize her with nicknames, who respected her work but more so respected the vision of her balancing two phones against her cheekbones in a busy newsroom, the way her fingers moved on a keyboard, the top button of her white linen dress that she wouldn't notice had come undone.

He called her "champ" and "scoop," made efforts to be well-informed of her story assignments. He stopped by her desk with coffee, which she smiled and drank, but when he offered his help—I know a guy who such-and-such down at the so-and-so who could really—she was curt and unreceptive.

After four months of working there, she finally agreed to have a drink with him and some other guys from the paper in celebration of the triumphant finish of a particularly rough deadline. He made the mistake of guessing her drink—surely a woman looking like her wanted something that suggested it tinkled and didn't stain—she snorted. What then, Scoop, he joked, scotch? She accepted, and my father and the two other reporters watched in silence while she took the full brown body in her mouth in one swallow. As my father tells it, that sealed the deal then and there.

It was another month before my mother agreed to go out with just him. My father felt, for the first time in his life, unsure of his approach with a woman. She seemed unaffected by the traces of his drawl that so many females adored (the way he, for example, still called his days "Sundee," "Mondee," etc.), the pointed dress shoes he kept polished but not gleaming, the well fitting corduroy blazers with leather patches on the elbows, the ever-present pencil placed jauntily on his ear and through his thick wheatbrown hair, the perfectly delivered wink. Maybe the third time he asked her out and flashed his famous perfect smile, she had replied: What? I'm supposed to congratulate you on your big old teeth? (But the way she said it, he insists, was somehow not derisive. It was even, almost, pleasant.)

It was Friday. They were to go for dinner after work. My father was unusually transfixed by the glow of the Xerox machine, spilled coffee in the break room and took extra time to clean it up, returned to his station and made all the calls he should have, and still there were hours left in the workday. Usually, from a diagonal across the newsroom, he could see a sliver of her desk from his, but today there was some obnoxious cat figurine or mug that blocked it. When it was finally six, he crossed the newsroom. The people remaining were typing frantically; the cartoonist had his curly head down, bits of eraser flying violently off his station with quick brushes of the stubby, ink-stained hand.

His heart sank when he reached her desk. She was still enmeshed. Surrounding her were yellow legal pads in various states of distress, clippings from their paper and others, a bit of lettuce and near it some crumpled wax paper, a stack of books, different makes of pens all showing signs of being savagely chewed on. Her glance up to him was a vague assimilation of an apology. He took off his blazer, took out something to read from the leather satchel he carried under one arm, and found a chair to sit on. He realized he had not eaten since eight that morning and made every effort not to look up at the row of clocks displaying the different times in Tokyo, London, New York.

At ten after seven he filled with joy as she began to stack things and put them away in the metal desk's drawers, wrapped a light silk scarf around her neck, put the last of a packet of crackers in her mouth and threw away their plastic wrapping along with the lettuce and the wax paper. She mouthed something to herself as she inventoried the contents of her oversized purse, she pulled the ball chain of the iconic green-cased lamp, she stood and beamed at him briefly.

She walked ahead of him to the elevator; she beat him at pressing the button that would bring them to the lobby and out of the building. He was to follow her in his car to a restaurant she knew. She was a terrible driver, and he

watched as she failed to signal, changed lanes without reason, drove too close to people, honked at red lights. Her
slender wrist emerged and withdrew from the driver's side
window when she flicked her cigarette.

She had chosen a soul-food place with a wooden front
porch and chairs that rocked and strings of heavy white
bulbs that crisscrossed over the tables. She insisted on sitting outside, though the night was certainly not warm and
nothing like the wet, dense Southern heat that the restaurant's ambiance implied so heavy-handedly and that my father knew and my mother didn't. She talked and listened
with a rare balance and got gravy all over her face. When my
father proffered his neatly folded handkerchief, she seemed
touched by a gesture so old-fashioned, and took it gladly.

What was said? These are the details my father strains
more to recall. She told him about her life and he told her
his. Her father was a lawyer; her father was a drunk; she
had found her brilliant older sister dead by her own brilliant hands when she was seventeen. Before college she
lived in Yosemite for a while, cleaning cabins, swimming
naked, taking and posing for photographs that later would
go into an album titled THE FUN CLUB.

By the end of the meal they were both sufficiently
drunk, she hooting and clapping her hand over her
mouth as if in shock, he cackling and telling stories with
his hands, using forks and knives as props. He insisted
on driving her home and laughed at the way she stuck
her head out the window like a dog, happy to feel air on
her booze-warm face. He thought her somehow more

beautiful red nosed and slightly sloppy. To his amaze-
ment, she invited him in.

After a nasty incident in which my father made the mistake
of sowing one last wild oat with a secretary from the floor
below who called him "dear," my mother did not return
his desperate answering machine messages, did not look
at him in the break room, and certainly did not express
thanks for the books and flowers he left at her house. But
for reasons my father can't supply, she finally gave in and
then it seemed they were together for better or worse. As
beautiful as she was, as hungry as she was, my mother had
reached a point similar to my father's at which she looked
around and realized she'd had enough fun. After only four
months, they leased an apartment together. She committed herself to domestic life, cooking terrible dinners, painting flea-market purchases yellows and blues, adding art to
the walls of the absurdly long Victorian hallway to make
it seem less like the brothel it once was. They bought a
Siamese cat who was pretty thoroughly unpleasant to be
around and made a habit of clinging to the walls and hissing, who is still alive somehow, and whom my father has
always insisted he loves.

When she became pregnant six months later, my father,
who figured he had missed the paternal boat, was ecstatic.
He took many photographs of her belly growing rounder
in the bathtub, on the plastic chaise longues set up on the
roof of their apartment. In these pictures she looks both

happy and thirsty, pretending not to smile; the city behind her winks in the sunlight, as if in on the joke.

Like so many parents, mine wanted to create for me the life they never had and began scouting for a quieter place to plant themselves. Having just inherited a neat sum of money from the death my grandfather, they were able to finance the small house in the small town bisected by a river of the San Francisco Bay where I would live and my mother would die.

The day following James and Jackson's unknowing suggestions toward a place where I could reach my mother, I woke early, stepping over the gnarled oak branches and cracks in the sidewalk, although my mother was dead and had no back to break. I quietly opened my front door, ran a bath, used the soap bar of my father's that left my skin dry and pine scented, braided my hair, listened to the snaps and crackles of my cereal, and packed my mother's dilapidated messenger bag. The walkie-talkies went in the safest pocket. Next, my father's fishing pole, poking awkwardly out from beneath the left flap, a roll of tinfoil, and two silver capes James and Jackson had left on my bedroom floor. I remember feeling, then, a rare sense of faith and control derived from both the arranged materials and the magic the boys' sleep had produced.

James and Jackson had only just woken when I crawled back in their window. Already, Jackson, whose mother liked to say would have gray hairs before she did, was rubbing his eyes and sighing as he resurveyed James's damage to the circus, demanding when, precisely, his little brother had witnessed a monster at a circus.

The astronaut clock that made satisfying rocket noises on the hour read ten fifteen. By eleven thirty, we were pink faced and moist, trudging down the tracks of the railroad that hadn't run in years.

Jackson and I walked ahead of James, him lagging behind to poke dead birds and using a found stick as a cane. I did not share my inspiration with Jackson, and he didn't ask after my strange quiet that day. I slowed my pace as we approached it, and the chalky dust rose around my ankles. I had seen it two weeks before, when my father's car had started making unsettling pinging noises as we crossed the freeway overpass. He broke into his strange brand of expletives ("Well I could just shit" is one I've never been able to explain); I got out of the car to witness the excitement and dramatics, and happened to look down at what majesty the freeway carried us over.

The abandoned railroad trestle I'd seen from safety above now stood in front of us, its up-close reality leaning in too many directions in too many places. The planks were not placed evenly, some had fallen, and the guardrails on either side clung grimly to their name, bending as if to meet the river halfway in compromise. A man slept at the edge of the water, ten feet below us, on a pillow of grocery store bags.

I offered James and Jackson their capes and motioned for them to sit down, placed the contents of my bag in a neat row, and asked Jackson to fasten one walkie-talkie as bait to the fishing line. Next, we tore three large pieces of tinfoil off the roll and set about constructing three crowns. I had no good reason for this, except the hope that it would cast us as more regal, more deserving, more capable of conducting electricity through our small bodies.

We held hands and assumed our positions against one of the rails; I delivered instructions as they stood and gaped at the filthy river. Above us, the highway made the sounds it does, whisking people away and bringing them back.

The fishing pole was too heavy for James on his own, so Jackson helped him lean the middle of it through the second rung of the guardrail. As the fishing line descended, it jerked with the weight of the walkie-talkie radio. James remained a king in his crown, noble and devoted to the good of his country.

At my count, Jackson and I began to sing. Although Jackson didn't know the implications of this song, I did. Knew them in every part of my breastless, motherless body. As verse moved to chorus, I became louder and more desperate, pressing my lips to the blue plastic. I sang like my father while he tenderly washed brick red plates and worn wooden spoons. It was an old Irish folk song he had taught us, that my mother's Irish uncles had taught her; because it was about a woman named Mollie, I understood it as written for my mother. The song is about a faraway city and a dead woman, once beloved, who died suddenly, still haunts the streets with a wheelbarrow full of mussels for sale. My father loved it for obvious reasons.

When the song was over, I pressed my ear to the radio, hoping for some sort of aquatic transmission from the ghost I was singing for. Jackson and I took turns listening. I paced up and down the bridge, hoping ghosts got reception three steps northwest. They didn't.

At five thirty, we stood where we'd started, silent. Even James was disappointed, though he couldn't tell why. He was the first to step down from the throne, then me, then Jackson.

The crowns bobbed as the river slowly pulled them past the homeless man, who had switched his face away from the bottles of urine.

Their father's face is clear in my mind from the photographs that surfaced once Jackson and James were "old enough," but I do not recollect any of the times he showed up on our street to smile and squint at James and Jackson through his thick Buddy Holly–esque glasses.

The pictures of Thomas are of a birdlike man dressed in ill-fitting suits, thin ties, and sharply angled dress shoes. He looks both embarrassed by and friendly toward the camera, and seems always to be leaning: it's like all the objects of the world constantly presented themselves to him in support. The sun often in his blue eyes, which are so light they seem almost diaphanous. He has the slight smile of a person who is in on a joke you are not.

Jackson later put up a photo of him in our apartment. It came not out of a sentimental place or an effort to miss someone he barely knew, but rather a black humor that most found disturbing but I, as someone who was also parentally ghosted, found hilarious. In it, Thomas is nearly

literally dancing on a grave. The background is a Confed-
erate cemetery he stopped by on a road trip at twenty-two
or so; he has his hands out on either side of him, a bottle
of beer dangling somehow from between the middle and
index fingers of his left hand. His right hand is four inches
higher, his feet placed one in front of the other. The photo
is taken from the back, and the wings of his coat indicate
motion; he doesn't know there's a picture being taken, but
his face is turned just enough to indicate he is smiling.

Jackson had it blown up to a 14-by-16 and hung it between the two windows we frequently kept open despite
the weather. The enlargement resulted in a graininess,
and friends or acquaintances visiting our apartment for
the first time liked to cluck their tongues and remark how
striking it was, sometimes even going so far as to assume
it was this writer or that artist captured by such and such
a photographer. On one occasion, when the asker was
particularly thoughtful and mistakenly convinced of her
cultural awareness, when she went so far as to insist she
knew the image of this obscure poet walking on a graveyard and had seen it in a gallery in London, Jackson and
I looked at each other and laughed, inclusively, at length.
When we finally calmed down enough to explain that the
washed-out image was no poet but rather just the long-
dead, drug-addled father of Jackson here, no one thought it
was very funny. Many people don't understand, I suppose,
that while respecting the dead is important, it's not always
easy and it's generally pretty boring.

What we perceived as an enmity between our parents was not quite that—though Julia often sold it that way. There were feuds and sideways looks, snippy comments to us about the other's parenting that we were meant to deliver. A couple times, when we were younger, our parents had taken battle stances on our respective front porches and hollered. It would always be pretty late when it happened, and the neighbors' windows would light up, slow and weary, like the sighs they were no doubt emitting in their bed- and living rooms. The fights always concluded with my father more amused than angry, delighted at Julia's easy female temper, and her, livid, slamming things around in the kitchen pretending to be looking for something—but when Thomas was found dead in a flophouse in Oakland when Jackson was eight and James almost seven, it was my father who took Julia to identify the body and bring her glasses of yellowish water as she cataloged the erratic and strange evidence that her children's father had left behind. Perhaps my father was remembering that it had been Julia who stayed with him the first hour in our house without my mother, who had made him coffee and sensed he didn't want to talk and instead put on a Neil Young record she knew (somehow) he liked, soft but not so soft he couldn't hear the generosity of the words: *Will I see you give more than I can take? Will I only harvest some?*

It was this never-ending series of owe-you-ones that bound them together even beyond the fact of their children's hips being attached. Because they'd seen each other at their worst, I think, they felt relieved to leave those moments where they were—bury them in the dirt as opposed to making them a foundation. It was beautiful in the sad, secret way illicit affairs are: relationships that choose what to include, that are shaped only by the circumstances the participants experience together. It allowed, from what I can tell, my father to sustain a picture of himself he more or less liked: jaded and cynical but resilient, always willing to tell or hear a good joke. As for Julia, I can't say exactly what it gave her, only that the times I secretly glimpsed them drinking coffee at our kitchen table, she seemed to hold herself differently, her shoulders lower, and spoke in soft peals I'd never imagined could come from her and found quite lovely.

They had quite a bit in common, given their dead spouses and the children they'd been left to raise alone in a town that had grown to overflow with nuclear families with two Volvos that escorted their sons and daughters to not only baseball but also piano and art lessons. Only my father had learned to laugh at these people, and Julia secretly envied them; she cursed her shotgun wedding to the man who, with the arrival of the second young, grabby boy, ran off quicker than you could say child support.

"Irony" is a word I hesitate to use. My life has been marked, dyed, twisted, by the unexpected or inconvenient, and any safe patterns I could identify would seem forced. In any case, when my father and Julia essentially united after Jackson and I separated, "irony" certainly seemed to be the word the rest of the world wanted to employ. It was something of a concession on both of their parts, but they seemed oddly happy to make it.

Were they dating? I asked. Not exactly. They had simply decided that officially being on the same team seemed to make sense. Julia put her house on the market (it sold in a matter of days) and moved the few doors down into my old bedroom. My father had been diagnosed with emphysema three years before, and the disease was starting to close in. He took the invasion gracefully and with wonder; he was amazed at the ways his body, of which he was so long the master, started submitting to another owner. Julia supervised his breathing exercises, took walks around the block with him, refilled his prescriptions at the pharmacy, grew to love the finicky, aging cat. They cooked elaborate dinners that they ate before the flickering of the Turner Classic Movies channel; she revived my father's garden while he watched from a chair set up in the sun. They swapped sections of the newspaper over breakfast, they played Scrabble with my father's house-sized *Oxford English*

Dictionary open and ready. Julia took on the domestic role wholeheartedly as she'd never done before: she sewed new curtains of panels of sheer pastels for the living room, she painted their mailbox yellow, she wore floppy sun hats and made sun tea. Talking to my father on the telephone was like a three-way conversation, him often repeating to Julia what I'd just said, or me waiting while they laughed their way through a private joke.

I was happy for them, though I couldn't help but feel strange that after Jackson had cut-and-dry removed himself from our long-woven history, our parents had found a way to enforce it. We had so long kidded about them getting together, but when they actually did, he wasn't around to balk at the punch line.

It crossed my mind whether it would have happened if we'd stayed together, whether it had been pending awhile but their children being romantically linked had prohibited even the discussion. And if it had, was it better that Jackson and Ida—a dangerous, circuitous affair that had festered too long—had ended, so They could begin? Did the factually old deserve more than those who simply felt too aged for their own good?

Eventually the circus came down in favor of other projects, ones requiring less devotion and planning. Jackson was happy with build-your-own wooden planes and ant farms, and relieved of a good amount of guilt. The circus had remained on the walls through fall and winter, some pieces of the butcher paper curling and estranging themselves from others. Though he had tried, on many occasions, to make progress, the fine markings of his pencil, erased and redrawn, only looked alien and insignificant next to the seven giant chartreuse sharks James had carelessly slopped on in crayon one afternoon. The permanence of the wax frustrated Jackson; the jagged triangular teeth teased the procession of small dogs through a hula hoop he had taken such pains with.

I had tried to help, my hair held back by yellow heart barrettes. I drew a cage around the misshapen sharks, but that black wasn't thick or powerful enough, only made the beasts seem sort of striped, and that, to Jackson, was even worse. So in the spring, after much deliberation, he admitted defeat.

His mother noticed a certain adultness in the way her son devoured his after-school peanut butter and jelly; when he was finished, he cleared his throat and locked himself in the bedroom. In the hour and a half James was at his swimming lesson, taking immense pleasure in his green goggles and floating, Jackson took the pieces down, one by one, and placed them in a box until he decided what to do with them. He trusted I would come up with something. He looked forward to his brother's return, expecting screams and sobs, to an expression of passion their project had deserved but James had never provided.

What he got was almost worse. James did not acknowledge the absence, didn't notice how bare their wall suddenly seemed, how the paint previously beneath their doomed circus was a shade brighter than the rest of it. Instead he flopped onto his bed, demonstrated his perfected breaststroke, and made gurgling sounds into the cowboy sheets. Jackson was furious. That night, he lay awake with a knotted stomach while James dreamed and murmured.

"Everyone . . . can have the peanut butter," said James's sleep, and Jackson began to unknot as he hoped for a brilliant revenge.

Though Jackson was generally very attentive in school, thrilled by mathematical equations and more so by their answers, that Friday he mostly drew circles, over and over until they perforated the paper. On the walk home he stepped on every crack and did not participate in the game of slug bug that James and I played halfheartedly. James, sensing something the matter, wondered amiably what was for dinner to an apathetic Jackson. As he watched us pass, the old man who always sat on his porch in pleated dress pants, puffing at his pipe, was thankful for another spring, especially watching James shoot finger guns at the passing cars. We were encouraged not to speak to strangers, but when the old man asked us how we were on our walk home every day, we smiled in the best way we could think of.

Today, though, Jackson gave no notice.

My father found the Godzilla in the bottom of a box at a yard sale three months before, hidden beneath some children's books whose illustrations had been edited with crayon, and held it up to James, who shot out his arms in welcome immediately. It wasn't priced, wasn't supposed to be there, and the woman with untouched roots in unflattering pink capri pants, whose children were long gone from Madrone Street, shrugged and said she'd take whatever they gave her. My father pulled out a dollar; James found a filthy gumball-machine toy in his pocket, one of those sticky hands made of gel material that flew and stretched with a flick of the wrist, and offered it to the woman, who just smiled morosely at her magazine and told him to keep it.

While my father's gesture was kind, it only gave Julia more reason to dislike him; nothing in the house was safe from Godzilla. Besides the expected destruction of minia-ture cities, he devoured the petals from the flowers that sat in a vase by the kitchen window, he tore down shower curtains (despite being only eight inches tall), he tormented the cat, he microwaved earrings, he disrupted the meticulous organization of Jackson's underwear drawer, he overflowed the bathtub.

"It was Godzilla" became James's catchphrase, and he went as far as to scorn the toy in front of his mother. She was not fooled: the monster slept with him every night. With time the house grew relatively peaceful again, with only the occasional pile of folded laundry strewn or a splattering of "blood" on the front door. Now Godzilla spent most of his time guarding the beta fish (who were not concerned for their safety either way). Though James's appetite for destruction had cooled, the Godzilla remained adored and admired; he liked the shadow of the monster cast on his wall by the night-light.

Because Jackson had always been privately jealous of the Godzilla, and played with it in secret, casting the doll as a gentle giant who sang to the smattering of tiny cowboys and Indians and carried hurt G.I. Joes to rescue in its mouth, he knew it well. It was of an older design, its claws likely hand painted, with hard bumps on its plastic to represent gruesome skin. A seam ran down its face, its protruding stomach, down the tail, and up the back.

The task would require a surgeon's precision, but Jackson was confident and appointed me as his assistant. I watched as Jackson took a pillowcase from the linen cabinet and placed it over the Godzilla, covering its head first. From the kitchen he took a knife his mother used for chopping vegetables and a jar of peanut butter, placed them both in the pillowcase, and we headed out the back door.

I was conflicted, but Jackson was so intent, his eyes so needy, that I agreed to help. We decided my living room had the best light and the most space, and placed lingerie ads and classifieds on the hardwood floor to reduce the likelihood of evidence. I held the monster's arms down while Jackson considered his best angle, deciding finally that throat to crotch would be the easiest. The first jab required more pressure than he thought, but after a couple tries it came easier; the knife aligned itself to the seam nicely as Jackson sawed in and out of the hard plastic.

"Peanut butter," said Jackson, who watched hospital dramas with his mother.

"Check."

"Spoon," commanded Jackson with a grimace.

"Check."

A smooth curve of the metal worked initially, but to really pack the monster's guts, Jackson realized he would have to use his hands. When all the hollow spaces of the stomach were filled, Jackson pressed the seam back together, delighted at what an adhesive the peanut butter had turned out to be. It wasn't apparent, either, unless you were up close, that the creature had been operated upon. With ten minutes until James returned glowing from backstrokes, Jackson and I hurried back to his house and placed the monster in its original position. The sunlight of four thirty p.m. slanted perfectly in through the window, threatening playfully to ooze the innards of James's Godzilla.

I was pleased and proud, and I felt the sensation of Us so strongly that I reached for his hand and squeezed it. What I felt were words I didn't know yet, words like "clammy" and "trembling." Even when you are so young, seeing a child suppressing his tears, biting his lip, is strange. It is at this age we are allowed to feel generally how we like, and so to be ashamed, to begin to view one's emotional outpours as events that would be judged, was odd. I let go of Jackson's hand, shocked, and his quaking gave way to sobbing.

Ultimately, it was Jackson who ended up squeezing the peanut butter out of the monster, Jackson who was made ignoble by something destroyed by his own hand. Remembering him and the splayed-open, exploding figure, it is clear he loved it just as much as his brother had; it is clear he loved it for how much James had loved it, by proxy of loving James; it is clear he hadn't wanted to hurt anything that amounted to love, that he hadn't seen the equation clearly.

I know my mother because my father has given her to me. As concession for her not being around, he racked his brain for details that would soothe the lack, that would give me proof beyond photographs that she had existed. As such, they are the closest I have to memories of my mother, and though I cannot attest to witnessing her as an obscenely messy eater, I can smile upon the discovery of ketchup on my blouse and insist happily on its passed-down origin.

There is one story my father could not tell me, so I told it to myself: my mother in a loose nightgown, her hair falling around her, groggy, looking out the window that morning. She opened the refrigerator and noted that like always, milk was low but butter in excess. She was troubled by a dream the contents of which she couldn't recall, only the unsettling conclusion. I had just learned to crawl and her body was tired from chasing me. There are variables, of course—what, exactly, was different about the way she took her coffee cup down from the cupboard so that her hip rubbed the knob on the oven? How long did it take before she knew, and did she, with a distance she recognized as strange, for a moment find the lapping of the flames beautiful?

The memory I have, which I know is not a memory but rather something my brain horrifically constructed over and over again during my childhood, shows my mother between the stove and counter, a tight space a foot and a half wide, trying to get a better look out the highest window, which was small and situated unusually high. In some versions she is spying on our neighbor, a lonely, funny man named Warren my father later befriended as a solitary man himself; sometimes she is watching our cat's slow attack of a bird. She turns because she thinks she's heard me cry out in my sleep, forgetting her proximity to the stove.

The fire travels up the light cotton to the neckline (the material stretched with my tiny hands), catching on its way her hair, which is almost the same color as the flames. Her first reaction is slow; she just looks down and watches as her body grows warmer than it's ever been, than she ever thought possible. She holds her palms out incredulously, she calls for my father, she notices for the first time that the too-bright yellow they painted the kitchen is something she loves fiercely, not just pleasant but *exquisite*. She calls for my father, she whirls, she remembers vaguely to drop to the ground but it seems as if the heat is lifting her, she is overwhelmed by the smell her hair is making. The cotton is clinging to her as if another layer of skin; she is impressed by how quickly something foreign has become a part of her. She calls for my father. At this point, I am crying.

She calls for him, but he cannot hear her. His great hands clutch at lilac flannel sheets as if clinging to a rope; the sweet smell of liquor clings to him cloudlike, fermenting. In the kitchen, the flames have reached around to heart and lung. His mouth forms an O, waiting for the dream's punctuation. It is Warren, our neighbor, who smells the smoke rising from my mother's flesh and climbs in through the bottom window always left a crack open for the cat and calls 911 and rises my father, whose dreams have left him with an erection that falls promptly while he holds my mother's limp and growing limper hand.

Since then my father has had difficulty sleeping, no matter how high the dosage of the sleeping pills or whiskey or a brief phase of cheap white wine that I gently teased him about. I grew used to his silhouette in my doorway, his eyes squinting to make out the rising and falling of my chest. Sometimes, I would wake to see him sitting at my desk, tinkering with the loose knob on the third drawer down or straightening my schoolbooks into piles; once, he had opened my algebra textbook and begun solving equations. I pretended to keep sleeping and hoped, for his sake, that he could find n.

When he calls late at night and feigns that there was something he was supposed to tell me but can't remember just now, I pretend, for his sake. For mine, too.

The fall that followed the circus, the kidnapped girl from around the corner came to me in dreams on a yellow bicycle with a banana seat and streamers of thousands of colors. I was always waiting on the porch for her, feeling the cool stone against the part of my thighs my shorts didn't cover, but when she came she was anxious and I'd always forgotten to get my bicycle from behind the house where I kept it, or my father began calling me from somewhere inside only to deny it once I'd found him. By the time I was on my bicycle, she was at least a block away, looking back at me with the half smile in the picture on all the missing posters. But in the dreams my calves strained, as if I were riding up a steep incline; there was grit in the air that caught in my throat and settled on my skin, adding pounds. The streets I knew had different names or didn't intersect like they should, and while I struggled to keep up she weaved effortlessly, waving at the people I didn't recognize, riding with no hands, showing off.

Within two full days of her disappearance, the case attracted national publicity. I was eye level with the magazine rack in the grocery store, and her face looked back at
me from all the magazines; it was hard to understand that
these were glossy pages being sold across the country, that
any pain or person could exist past the limits of the park at
the corner or even the diner on the boulevard with high,
spinning seats that took an eternity to drive to. I wondered
what it felt like to be a girl everywhere; I thought that if I
was in her place, I might feel lucky.

When I told my dad this on the way home from the
market, he grew very quiet and turned off the radio. He
didn't even respond when I saw a red Volkswagen pass and
punched him in the shoulder. At home he sat me on the
couch without even unloading the groceries, and I tried
hard to listen and not think of the milk sitting in the trunk
growing warmer. Dear heart, my father said, Anna is not
lucky.

Did I understand what kidnapping was? A very bad person had taken Anna. He had come into her bedroom with
a knife during a slumber party. He had tied her two friends
up and put pillowcases over their heads. He had told them
to count to a very high number and carried Anna out of
the bedroom. Was that lucky? His throat caught and he put
his face in his hands.

They weren't sure where she was now, my father explained. Her mom and dad and the police were looking
very, very hard, and so were many other people. There was
a candle lit in the window of her house that would stay lit

until she returned. We could walk by and see it anytime I wanted. Would I like to bring flowers?

In the days and weeks that followed, I as well as the rest of the children in the neighborhood lost that sense of ownership we'd felt over the summer. FBI agents came knocking at the door, searching for information, holding up the flyer that was everywhere already. We were not allowed to walk home from school alone; I was not to walk to James and Jackson's without an escort; my bedroom window was to remain closed and locked at absolutely all times; my door was to be left open. We were taught the term "stranger danger." All vans white or even close to white in color were viewed as ominous—they being the official vehicle of Kidnappers and Bad Men everywhere—and fictional reports of seeing them echoed excitedly before the bell that signaled the start of class.

Anna was four years older and had just begun junior high. Though she was too old to join in on our games, she would sometimes smile encouragingly when she walked or rode past. She was thin and lanky like I was, with unruly brown hair she always wore in unkempt waves and wide red lips that curved over the gap in her slight front teeth. She wore baseball shirts with three-quarter length sleeves; on the few times I was close enough, she smelled to me like soaked-in chlorine and the thick, unpasteurized apple juice my father bought in the spring. I had spoken to her only a handful of times, which I replayed in my head obsessively. On the Fourth of July two months before, I had shared a whole ten minutes near her: she had taken the empty canvas camping chair next to me, placing a soda can in its mesh cup holder and adjusting her fascinating preteen body with little sighs. Eager to impress her, I had mentioned how one time Jackson and I had got our hands on some illegal fireworks from Chinatown in San Francisco, leaving out the fact that Julia had confiscated them almost immediately. Anna had beamed briefly, politely, and emptied her soda can, the last of the cola tinkling as it escaped into her lips. In the middle of the street, my father lit a foot-tall brick and held his beer bottle up triumphantly as it rained its bits of slow, mournful yellow lights twelve feet above.

"As much as I like the fireworks," Anna said then, "I like the smell afterward," and sniffed as if to demonstrate. I couldn't think of any response, and soon after she got up, leaving the aluminum can and a wake of her scent.

It wasn't just Anna that had been stolen. The drugstores raised their Halloween aisles from wherever they'd been hiding for a year, and our street bore less and less resemblance to the kingdom we'd galloped through laughing and planning wildly. Autumn was decidedly adult: the nuanced colors—muddled oranges and browns, the uncertain gray of the clouds—were much harder to love, to understand, than the sticky pinks of popsicles, the confident thick greens of happy grass and plants, the haughty blue of the sky above it all. I halfheartedly indulged my father's conversations regarding my costume that year, and on the night when the boys and their mother came over to carve pumpkins on our porch, I was distracted and without my usual grandiose jack-o'-plans. I took pleasure, instead, in making deep, sharp stabs, cutting only sharp lines and extracting simple shapes from the flesh of the pumpkin, and removing its guts in fistfuls.

The man who'd taken Anna had waved a knife at her friends: I wondered if somewhere he was making similar incisions, stealing her flesh in isosceles triangles and parallelograms. In my imagination this was not painful for Anna, only confusing; she would look at her body and watch the light coming through, then behind her at strange shadows she cast. As a child who'd lost her mother, I had developed a morbid and skilled imagination regarding death and human pain that I felt somehow entitled to use.

The candle went on burning in the window of the Martins' house, and on the night of Halloween her parents sat on the porch with candies of every variety: nougat and fruit-flavored hard candies, peanut butter cups in milk and dark chocolate, lollipops with blue gum inside them. Instead of cauldrons of dry ice, ghoulish motion detectors that cackled on a trick-or-treater's approach, or an excess of gauze spiderwebs, their stoop was a tribute to the possibility of actual death. The flowers had not stopped coming and the bouquets bled into each other among store-bought sympathy cards and ones made of construction paper in seventh-grade homerooms: WE MISS YOU ANNA. Photographs cataloging twelve years of life were papered to the windows, the same smile replicated in different poses and ages.

Parents had to drag their children up the stairs; some of the littler ones cried. It was strange that her parents had done this; it was courageous or it was insane. Anna's mother wore a sedated smile, clutching the hands of parents and hungrily eyeing the cowboys and grim reapers; her father distributed candy in businesslike gestures, nodding and drinking out of a red plastic cup. When we approached, my father offered his hand but I shook it off. I maintained eye contact with the mother of the stolen girl until she broke it; I felt Jackson staring from beside me and cast him a look of reprehension.

As per routine, I spent Halloween night in the boys' bedroom, where we traded caramel apple pops for watermelon Jolly Ranchers. James, with his unusual taste for the unpopular black licorice, gathered a wealth of them in his corner. His plastic pirate sword lay forgotten as he counted and recounted, until finally Julia came in and gave us ten minutes to change and brush our teeth and turn off the lights. From outside came the whoops of teenagers, the sudden acceleration of cars driven by those with new licenses, the *wee-woos* of a mechanical ghost slowly losing batteries.

The sources of light in their bedroom after dark were of a different frequency: the glow-in-the-dark stars stuck to the ceiling, the luminous crack from beneath the door that changed in color while Julia watched television, the modest glow of the fish tank, the red of the numbers from the astronaut clock—they were known by few and as such I cherished them as secrets, like the little sighs that issued from James like exclamations as he drifted off : *mm, mmph, Mmph!*

I couldn't sleep and whispered to Jackson to see if he was awake. I twisted my body toward him, I dared myself to ask the question that hung over the flowers and cards on the porch of the woman with the lost daughter:

"Where do you think she is?"

"I . . ." Jackson stuttered with the thought of I, with the thought of an authoritative statement; as children we were rarely asked questions of this gravity.

"I don't know. Maybe he let her go somewhere. Or maybe he wanted someone to come with him somewhere, and they're almost there, and *then* he'll let her go."

"Like where?" I tried to imagine Anna and a faceless man in a car, listening to the radio loud and stopping at gas stations so she could get whatever snacks she wanted, but I couldn't shake my vision of Anna with all the pieces missing, like what is left after the cookies have been cut out of the dough.

"Mexico?" I suggested. I had always liked the sound of Spanish being spoken by the Mexicans who waited around at gas stations for work: it seemed happy, the way it moved like mountains, rolling. There was a postcard from Puerto Vallarta on our fridge that I had memorized, and I imagined Anna in one of the beach lounge chairs, smiling that smile, sending little squirts of lemonade through the gap in her teeth or drawing a picture of the ocean: the reporters sometimes mentioned on television that art and music had been her favorite classes.

"Mexico. Yeah. Like maybe he was gonna go with his friend? But his friend couldn't? So he took Anna, only it's long-distance and she doesn't have the money to call."

Jackson rolled over and I looked, again, at the neon stars we had stuck to his ceiling, considering Mexico. I liked the idea that she was just on vacation, but *why her*? It had to be someone who knew her, who admired, like I did, the way her skin stayed brown and friendly all year, the way she tilted her head when she listened. Who maybe had seen her play piano at the band recital, like I had, and watched the way she bent her head way low and sideways, her curls falling even longer while her fingers leaped.

It wasn't long before James started murmuring, and as always, I was reassured by the sounds. They meant that people were still people when they slept, that these hours void of conscious words and sunlight were still part of the story, if perhaps in parentheses. And what fit between parentheses, I learned later, were often the parts that provided fuller meaning, that sought to include what was overlooked.

"The . . . the . . ." James struggled from his sleep, clearly on the verge of a pressing communication.

"THE COWBOY SKITTLES."

He lashed his head emphatically against the pillow, then reassumed inertia. I waited for Jackson's reply, but it never came. I cast my head to the astronaut clock, which read 9:17, and watched as the digital numbers changed, the backward and upside-down L becoming two boxes that signified 8. At 9:20, James let out a sharp breath.

"All night," Jackson said. "Gold."

"Nightgold," agreed James, his lips moving over his teeth between words. "All of it."

The clarity faded. The sleeping words deteriorated into syllables, and the syllables were like marbles scattering, rolling away from the others only to collide again as if happening into the same groove on their shared surface. The effect was that of someone imitating a language he didn't speak: it was nonsense that was grouped, punctuated.

"Ah za *kneeth*." It sounded as if James was pleading.
"Kerr pree, puh *hmz*."

"Miss-ing," sighed Jackson. "Missing missing."

"Missing," echoed James.

"Girl not lady."

"No-nowhere girl."

Seeing my opportunity, I butted in.

"Anna?" I asked. And then, more insistently, "*Anna?*"

"Anna," they breathed in unison.

"*Where?*" I demanded. "*Where?*"

"The man," began Jackson,

"walks bad," James asserted.

"Walks bad? Talks *bad*," Jackson clarified.

And then, in the rhythm of Morse code or telegrams, forms of communication obsolete and so fascinating in their urgency:

"Anna—gone—man—walks so bad—hiding."

I questioned Jackson the next day before school started. Had he had any dreams about Anna? None that he could remember, he said. And then, seeing the look on my face, his story changed: no, definitely not. But you *said her name*, I pleaded. He took his homework out of his backpack, put it on his desk, and looked up at the chalkboard. I was on my own.

As a little girl, I was normally comforted by mathematics, soothed by the premise of one true, right answer, but in the next few days the powdery white numerals against the dusty green were written, erased, rewritten, multiplied—and I hardly noticed. I also loved words—for an entirely different reason, for the way they lent themselves to endless combinations—but the spelling lists, also, I copied down with little interest and did not study later.

My father, like the rest of the parents, grew more distraught as the weeks went on and Anna never appeared. Except while the rest of them could almost believe the lies they told their children about it being only a matter of time before she was back helping her mother garden in the front yard, my father spent as much time as he could in the newsroom looking for the gruesome answer. He looked through pages and pages of local and surrounding areas' sex offenders, he reviewed the police report although he knew it by heart already, he read crime logs from the past six months, then a year and two years, but it was futile.

I made sense of it because I had to, or at least that is what I tell myself when the man's face appears in my memory: half paralyzed, something about the blue eyes sloppy but essentially kind. He was the janitor at the junior high school and sat almost every day at a sidewalk table of an Armenian café that served bottomless coffee, looking at nothing in particular and sometimes laughing rather convulsively at what the old men who also sat there said. Perhaps he had suffered a stroke at a relatively young age; he dragged the left side of his body dutifully, like an older brother chaperoning his younger sibling at the fair with effort, though not unhappily. He talked slowly and thickly and mumbled pleasantly to himself as he walked. Surely, I thought, he was the man who walked and talked bad that my sleeping friends had alluded to. Surely he had fallen in love with Anna as she breezily crossed the courtyard from fifth to sixth period, while he emptied the trash cans overflowing from the eighth graders' lunch. Surely he was hiding her.

Although I am cursed with a memory that forgives very little, the series of events that followed appear in matter-of-fact captions in my brain. The absence of typical floridity seems to imply that there can be no forgiveness for what I did. While my father was still at work, likely also sweating in the search to bring back Anna and what she'd taken with her of our little community, I called the number listed on the flyer and felt a strange giddiness at an action so independent. It was similar to the times my father had let me sit in his lap and steer; although his feet were on the brakes, I was happy to reign over the full circle of leather.

I supplied his name. They asked how old I was but still seemed willing to listen. When they asked what proof I had, I lied, though I had not planned on it. I said I had heard him talking to himself in the magazine aisle of the bookstore, picking up a glossy thing meant for young female teens and saying, "Anna will like this." It was a complex lie for someone so young to tell, and thinking about it now I am both impressed and disgusted.

They did not find the missing girl in his tiny in-law, but they did find cats. More than forty cats: some diseased, most inbred, of different colors, in different states of filth and malnutrition. The smell that occasionally came from the house, neighbors later reported, had been awful, but they'd had no idea about the animals. The cottage was far enough back from the street that the sound of the mournful, elongated meows and hissing had not reached the families eating quiet dinners, and the landlord reported that the man seemed friendly enough and always paid his modest rent on time. The footage of him on the news showed him in tears, and the papers reported him as dimwitted though remorseful. The number of cats had grown rapidly, from ten to seventeen in just a few months, and he had naïvely hoped he could love and take care of all of them. By the time the number had reached forty, the situation was long out of control, but he worried what would happen if he told anyone.

There were threats of charges and a slew of highly vocal animal rights activists, but in the end the former were dropped and the latter found causes less wilted and easier to chant slogans at than the lonely, possibly mentally disabled man who swept up thirteen-year-olds' messes.

I had never done anything to incite such a rage in my father. His anger took a subdued form that seemed to sit and percolate, wishing to avoid explosions, only outwardly expressing itself in a cupboard shut just too forcefully, a phone gripped just beyond necessity. The men in badges had come and given me a serious talking to, my father nodding in solidarity with his hands clasped between his knees. When they gave a roundabout implication that maybe I'd done this for the reward, I burst into hot, ignoble tears. They looked at each other and stopped. It was clear they'd said enough. My father shook their hands at the door and apologized again, closed the door, and laid his head, briefly, upon its frame. He took a brisk route into the kitchen, where he made a sandwich and left the ingredients sitting out. He spent the rest of the afternoon in his bedroom, and I tried to keep busy. I teased our unresponsive cat and rode my bike around the block fast and without pleasure; it became evening and my father had still not surfaced.

I wanted badly to see James and Jackson, but they were spending the weekend with Julia's mother in a dry, flat town four hours south. I was hungry. Though I was a reasonably autonomous girl and could easily have fixed myself something to eat, I did not. I reread part of a book about a brother and sister who run away to live in a museum and fell asleep with the light and all my clothes on, missing my mother fiercely.

I woke to the smells of breakfast and wandered into the kitchen, where my father gently asked that I sit. He put before me a heaping plate—a silent apology or an assimilation of one for not seeing to my dinner the night before—of two raspberry pancakes, two strips of bacon, and an egg-in-a-basket, the yellow-white a wondrously perfect circle against the even brown of the bread. He did not speak, did not look at me, and got up twice to refill his coffee. He did laugh lightly, perhaps sadly, certainly thinking of my mother, when a strand of my hair got into the syrup without my noticing.

I devoured every last bit. I was hungry from crying, from telling a useless lie, from what the missing girl had taken with her when she left, from the realization that had grown hard and final in my sleep: that she, and it, were not coming back. When he was sure I was done, he addressed me. We were to go to that poor man's house and I was, in no uncertain terms, to apologize. Furthermore, I was to have no more ideas about solving the mystery of Anna Martin. There were plenty of adults doing the best they could. I was to keep doing well on my tests, to ride my bike, to feel the independence and responsibility a library card afforded, to make thoughtful decisions based on my growing set of rights and wrongs, to do all the things Anna could not.

As we approached the man's little house and crossed the yard, which was thick with unraked leaves, I wished with all my concentration that he would not be home. As if he knew this, my father informed me that he had called Mr. Mortensen ahead of time and he was expecting us.

He opened the door in a pink pullover sweatshirt that was pilled and ill fitting and scared me, somehow. Though the cats had all been taken two days before, the smell was overwhelming. One sharp glance from my father let me know I was not to let the slightest acknowledgment of this so much as breeze across my face.

He looked at me, but not my father, with his down-turned and watery eyes.

"Come in . . . please," he said, with a slowness and thickness that sounded more like a muted foghorn than words. He shuffled in, gestured to a futon with sun-faded cushions so thoroughly defaced with cat scratches that the foam showed through more often than not, and sat himself in an orange plastic chair that was very clearly once the property of a junior high school classroom. The only other objects in the living room were a television, on top of it a bunch of little white flowers in a novelty plastic cup bearing a faded endorsement for a children's movie, and another school chair, but this one of dark blue. Tacked on the wall was a very old wedding photo-graph. The two people in the picture—presumably his parents—had their eyes slightly off center, and I tried to fixate on anything but that, the thought of him being a child once too much to bear.

"Ida?" My father asked. "Do you have something to say to Mr. Mortensen?"

The same hot tears began to stroll down my face. Tasting the warm salt in my mouth, I pushed my tongue against the roof of my mouth, willing the sibilant word I was here in this awful-smelling, sad excuse for a room to say.

"I'm suh, suh, sorry," I sobbed. "I wanted . . . I just wanted . . . her to be back."

The man gave me the look he probably received all day long, the look that says: *I pity you, but not quite enough to take the time to understand you.* He raised one hand, palm upward, and let it drop. He closed his eyes as if to make the vision of the lanky, crying girl go away. It was more than likely he wanted to share four walls with me as little as I wanted to share them with him. Neither the man nor I had the words for that moment, but my father did.

"Mr. Mortensen, I've explained the very serious consequences of her actions to my daughter, and she is, as you can see, extremely remorseful. I can't imagine what you must have gone through, and can only apologize again for the nightmare that was brought into your home."

The man, again, flipped his hand up in a gesture that could imply both receiving and offering. He nodded weakly, brought a remote from his pocket, and turned on the television. It was a signal as good as any, and we left.

Two weeks later, the case was solved—though "solved" seems the wrong word for it. (Were it solved, the girl would have been back in the neighborhood, all the photographs and votive candles would be taken off her porch, and our parents would not think twice if we were not home exactly within the ten minutes it took to return from school.) Though what all the parents wanted was for a broad-shouldered, fiercely virtuous detective type to come across a hidden clue that snapped all pieces together and led to the kidnapper, that was not what happened. There was no hero. Instead, a man with a criminal record that spanned years simply came forward and confessed. He had strangled Anna with a piece of yellow cloth, he said, and would lead them to her grave. The body had decayed for two months, but the blue-and-white-striped flannel pajamas Anna had been wearing served as instant identification. In the photograph that graced the front pages of all the newspapers, taken in the courtroom after the man was sentenced to death, he is smiling.

Though on paper I had only given local animal rights activists a cause to unite around briefly and community members an unpleasant aftertaste to gossip about, it seemed to Jackson that I had at least done *some*thing about the missing girl, and I think this is how he avoided the issue of my using what he may or may not have said in his sleep as a reason to go ruining the life of some poor disabled guy with a repulsive amount of cats—although years later, it showed up in his memory as an event altogether *wrong*, something he felt embarrassed to be even slightly connected to. What it did was make him think about consciousness in a way that children are hardly prompted to do. He'd pick things up just for the sake of dropping them; read aloud the backs of packages of macaroni and chicken pot pie his mother kept in the freezer, sounding out consonants; turn on the faucet to slight, medium, strong and feel the various pressures on different parts of his hand. All of these acts sacred, private, even beloved. He grew obsessed with navigation, pored over maps, saved up his allowance for a compass. It became very nearly a tic, the way he would take out the prized metal object and announce: *north. northeast. southw-southeast!* He urged us to try new routes to school, elaborate zigzags and "shortcuts"— *just a left, a right, and a sharp right.* More: he memorized the bones in his body in order to understand and own how they carried him. What felt like moments before, we'd felt a dumb pride in sticking needles into the thickness of our summer calluses, but now Jackson spoke in metatarsals and phalanges.

Burdened by a capacity he never asked for, Jackson began to process his ability to shift the world around him in his sleep without his specific desire and designed a reaction: he set about wanting small things and making them happen. Even if it meant pressing the doorbell and procuring the expected sound, the fact that he had made it happen, during the daylight, in his favorite thin red cotton shirt, felt important. When his mother regaled houseguests with stories of his sleepwalking and the adults cackled over the absurdity of, for instance, The Family Heirloom Jackson Put in the Fish Tank or The Time Jackson Tried to Put on a T-shirt as Pants, he felt so embarrassed that he had to leave the room. Oh, honey, his mother would say as he left, but she would continue to laugh and then offer her friends the even further hilarious anecdote of the time she found him allegedly using a roll of toilet paper as a telephone and asking more and more insistently to be connected to someone named Rick. Often the laughter at the Rick story carried enough that back in his room, he would stick his fingers in his ears and hum obsessively, or, if he let me, I'd lead us in song at increasing volumes, keeping in mind what my father told me: it's hard to know all the words, so the ones you do know, you've got to sing really loud.

Jackson was still at the age where praying could be a vagary, and before he slept he made bargains with whoever might accept them. Please, he breathed in and out, let me stay quiet and I'll be nicer to James. Let me stay in one place while I sleep and I'll never again ridicule my mother's cooking until she cries. Please.

The church around the corner from our street is long gone (at least in its identity as a church); for years it was left alone, the marquee blank and its plastic yellowing, although the drab add-on unit where the preacher and his family lived was rented briefly several times, always by single people who kept their curtains drawn behind the very small windows. Eventually a gay couple in their forties bought the building, oohing and ahhing at the high ceilings, laughing at the ironic potential of the altar, and envisioning many parties. They kept the windows open for days on end, letting out the smell of Christ, painting all the walls yellow and hand-oiling the floors with organic orange cleansers, shrieking with amusement, playing David Byrne or chaotic piano ensembles. But different sorts of noises began to echo out the windows, and the two gay men became one gay man who did not find the yellows to his suit anymore and certainly did not keep the windows open.

But: it *was* a church, and there was a preacher, and there was a preacher's daughter, and her name was Heather, and Heather was in the same grade as Jackson and me, and we did something bad to Heather.

She had the brand of eerily white-blond hair that does not get darker with age, skin just as pale, and slits of brown eyes. Her father had encouraged her to befriend the children in the neighborhood, after her arrival in the third grade, and she took a special liking to me. Perhaps because I lived with just my father, perhaps because I did not attend church, perhaps because I was fearless on the rope swing that hung from the oak tree in the front yard. I didn't want her around. I pushed her too high; she wrapped her legs tight around the two-by-six and squealed as if being held over a fire; I pushed harder and pretended to misunderstand her cries as joy.

Heather was always regurgitating bits of her father's sermons. Possibly she didn't yet believe them, but they were the only bits of conversation she had to make, and she wanted badly to be my friend. I was quick and vile in response, and Heather didn't seem to mind one way or another. It seemed to her that as long as both of us were making sounds, that meant we were bonding. She wanted to play innocuous games with my dolls. "Pretend," she would say, "pretend she has to go to a dance, but, but"—her imagination was for shit. "But *what*, Heather?" I'd reply. "But her house is on fire? But Spanish pirates are about to kidnap her?" It was no use. Heather just dressed and redressed the dolls, asked me what I thought of the *pink* shoes with the *blue* dress. When I complained, my father said I had to be nice to her, but I think he found the way her normalcy intricately tortured me privately amusing. At dinner when she said please and thank you and talked about heaven, he had to suppress a smirk while I notably slammed my milk glass, scraped my teeth on my fork, made fart noises in my elbow. "Stop, Ida," he said sternly, but later laughed until he cried and told me I was his favorite daughter. But I am your *only* daughter, I would say. That's right, he said with a firm furrow of the forehead, the *only one*. When he said "only," it meant something different.

Heather got the hint, or at least gave up trying. With the eventual relegation of dolls, the more complex math problems, the beginnings of breasts, Heather's insipid nature leaned more toward cruelty. We arrived at junior high school and she took to carrying a Bible with her in the hallways, even leading this as a trend of sorts among other girls in high-buttoning shirts and beige pants. When we passed she took to tilting her head in mock sympathy and God-blessing me, she and her comrades snickering in my wake. In classes she raised her hand frequently, fingered the cross around her neck and offered her thoughts, generally framing them as direct from her Father or her father. She declined to engage in certain required reading, brought notes from her dad that forbade her from doing so.

Adolescence had descended on us, though not without our knowing. Jackson and I didn't speak of the mysteries of antiperspirant versus deodorant, or the different kinds of underwear the girls in the locker room began to wear, but we related to each other differently, as if circling. We sat on my stoop but spoke of doing something else. We played catch from farther and farther distances down our street, and sometimes, watching the baseball land somewhere besides our mitts, neither of us went to grab it.

One of the first afternoons of spring that year, Jackson and I settled on my front lawn with our Spanish textbooks in our laps and conjugated verbs, learning all the different ways to eat, to listen, to cry, to run. Somewhere between past and present tenses, we lost direct contact with the newly returned sun and found Heather in its path there, blocking our warmth. She was clad in the deep sort of pink that looks good on no one, her backpack adjusted high up her shoulders.

Sensing my choice not to speak, Jackson did. "Hey," he went, without warmth.

"Hi, Ida." Heather spoke from her nose.

"I saw your father out walking late last night," she accused.

"He likes to do his thinking like that."

"My dad saw too. He says it must be hard on you."

I went back to quiet, poured my energy into I go, you go, she goes, we go, they go.

"Growing up the way you do. Your dad always working. He thinks it's not right, you spending all your time alone with those *boys*. But you know? I told him the Lord forgives you. Having basically no family and all. You're always welcome for dinner at our place, you know. It might be good for you to be around a father *and* mother. People who really care for your soul."

"Hey, Heather!" Jackson speciously enthused in the same voice he used when tricking James into doing his chores by some clever trade or another. "Wanna see something we just found? Out back?"

Her eyes lit up like she hadn't just been pushing at the weakest folds of my heart, and she followed him but immediately.

The tree outside our living room window was sickly and small, but it served its purpose. How long Heather remained hanging there, strung by her wrists and ankles by a string of Christmas tree lights, a bandanna tied around her mouth, I'm not sure. She did not cry out or protest, and right before Jackson covered her thin, pallid lips she asked God to save us.

"Shut up!" cried Jackson. "Shutupshutupshutup," his words coming fast like a metronome gone mad.

When I returned after dinner, terrified, the preacher's daughter was gone, the ghosts of tiny lights hanging in apostrophe of the day's events. I tore them violently from the branches, shaking boughs and loosening leaves, crossed the street, and placed them in my neighbor's garbage can. The thud of the black plastic lid falling behind me as I raced across the asphalt was deafening, and I expected every window on the street to fill with light as if to ask: *What are you doing? What have you done?*

Just as the first evening we spent tenderly examining each other's bodies—an act with implications we were far, then, from understanding—was never mentioned, neither was what we did to Heather, or what Heather did to me. In school she made every effort to pass by my desk, sometimes giving my hair a little tug; I would look up from a spelling test to find her looking at me, unblinking, and she would grin and grin and grin. I spent the months after that waiting for a knock at the door, or to be summoned into the living room to find my father and the preacher, a balding man with hairy, stubby hands, talking in low voices about me, about Heather.

The knock never came. One day Heather showed up at school with her arm in a sling and did not take unnecessary routes to pass by my desk; the next day she was gone. That Sunday a crowd gathered outside the church, waiting to be saved, speculating as to why the doors were locked.

For weeks and months, the marquee displayed the same message:

WE ARE

NOT PERFECT

JUST FORGIVEN

Some nights I listen to my ragged breathing and re-member: in the space behind my eyes, memories ap-pear Technicolor. Pink and yellow light shines through the visions in my half sleep, as if they were constructed of rice paper, and I try, with such an aching, to replicate the smell of chlorine, to recreate the laughter of those long gone, to set these stories in my head in stone so they can be done with.

Some nights I remember peaches. Tonight is one of them.

Jackson had a job at the market one summer. He was seventeen, I was almost. The sunflowers in the front of the store were larger than any I've seen since, and the an-cient cashier with the cigarette voice was named Paula. No: Linda. She called me rosebud and complimented my wrinkled sundresses. The bathroom was in the right front corner; it had only one stall and I can't remember what the hand soap smelled of but I promise myself I will before I

sleep. Jackson worked four days a week—or was it five—
and his work shirt was never clean. It smelled definitively
of him, even from where I would stand, across a display of
clementines touted for peeling easily. I pretended I was a
customer, crossed my arms and sighed over the selection
of fruits and vegetables.

But what's the *difference*, I whined as I fingered the donut
peaches, and he smiled patiently with the left side of his
mouth curving up like it had since we were kids. You see,
ma'am, if you can believe it or not, and he'd pause with
mock astonishment, these were cultivated especially for a
Chinese emperor—and now I can't remember the name of
the emperor but I decide I will, before I fall asleep. Never
mind the name. Remember the donut peach. You must, I
tell myself. Must.

They were cultivated for a Chinese emperor, Jackson
would say, who loved peaches but disliked the mess, so they
designed the *pan tao*, the flat peach, which fit right in between
his mustache and beard. It occurs to me between ticks that
he may have made this up. No, no, he couldn't have. Go on.

What about this one. I would say, it *looks* funny. Should
the skin look like that? All white like that? Don't judge a
book by its cover, ma'am, and he would laugh politely, this
here is the arctic white and I might say it's finer than the
rest of them. Oh, really? Why? Well, first you've got less
fuzz, he'd say, and I'd acknowledge this with a *huh* and hand
on my hip. They're just about the sweetest peach you'll get,
but they ripen more quickly, so you eat these guys up once
you get home, ma'am.

I force myself to remember, now lying on my side: free-stone: the flesh falls away from the pit when you bite into it. Clingstone: it refuses to.

Inevitably my peach facts run out and I lie awake, feeling unsettled, knowing that there's so much I'm forgetting. I get up.

In the bathroom I undress and examine myself. I arrange myself horizontally in the bathtub, and I turn the shower on and wrap my arms around myself, feel the water from its great height of origin. I try, this time, to remember nothing at all.

The first time we touched each other, I was seven, Jackson eight. My father, in a particularly good mood, had offered to take the boys off Julia's hands, take all of us to a swimming spot he knew of. She hated my father, or maintained that she did for a large chunk of my childhood, but there was nothing Julia valued more than a moment away from the physical and psychic tugs that issued from her sons' mouths day in and day out. (*T is for Tired*, read the alphabet book James would be assigned to write in school that year. *If we are bad Mom gets tired.* It was accompanied by a drawing of Julia, her hair in curlicues branching in every direction, her eyes the X's that signified dead, and three pink triangles that represented a bathrobe. In a moment of black humor she taped it to her bedroom door, and we heard her and a girlfriend cackling about it late one night in the kitchen.)

School had started, but the weather had not changed: an unbearable incongruity. In protest, I wore my blue bathing suit, which had begun to pill around the crotch, underneath the brand-new denim and gingham blouses my father had bought me for the first week of classes. The first days, as always, seemed like a sort of play: surely they were not asking us to add and subtract numbers when just days before we had reigned the uneven sidewalks with games that lasted after dark. My father was nothing if not indulgent, and sensing this, put us in his large boat-sized car with bouncy seats the Sunday before the second week began.

We made our way up the winding hills of Marin County, me sticking my head out the window pretending I was a happy golden Labrador, my father singing along to radio. Buddy Holly. *Every day, it's a-gettin' closer*: I could tell he loved that song, and had for a long time. James sang it: *Everyone says go ahead and catch her*, instead of *ask her*, as if it were a ballad of capture the flag.

We had to park on the edge of the road, which sat essentially on a cliff, and get out of the slightly tilted car on the side of traffic. We all chained hands and pretended not to be scared of the cars whizzing by, appearing from around the curves. The path down was sometimes uneven and at those points my father reminded us: "Three points of contact." That meant have at least one hand and two feet, or two hands and one foot, on the ground or a steady rock or whatever you can find. This phrase still comes to me, sometimes, my father's voice didactic but soothing. *Three points of contact.*

They were called the inkwells, the pools of water that flowed into ones below them by miniature waterfalls. We took turns jumping off the rocks into the deeper pools, marveling at being suspended, if briefly, in the air above the water. James played a secret game with himself up by the trees, his lips pursed and spitting sometimes as a result of dramatic sound effects. My father, treading water, placed his hands on the small of our backs while we floated and looked up at the early September sky: it was better, somehow, than our beloved August's and July's had been. I remember that moment as a blinking cursor, as if our buoyancy gave us the freedom, the permission we needed to press the boundaries we did that evening.

My father had taken us out only under the condition that we study for our spelling test that evening. We sat on the floor beneath the open window of the brothers' bedroom, still in our bathing suits, taking turns drilling one another, but my mind kept returning to Jackson sneaking up underwater and nibbling my toes.

"*S'hot*," he kept complaining. Tired of his whining and likewise heated, I removed my bathing suit, simultaneously proud and embarrassed. "Now you," I insisted. We balked at the silliness of our naked bodies and began the scientific exploration, sitting cross-legged on the carpet, parallels of gender and the entire universe as we understood it. What he had was much different from mine: I held it in my hand and let it drop, held it in my hand and let it drop. In retaliation he began to poke at me. Quick, tentative jabs, the tiny pink knob that would be with me forever listening, waiting. If this was wrong, it was only because, like our classmates taunted, *secrets don't make friends*, and this was certainly a secret.

Julia was in the kitchen, washing dishes, and James, we thought, asleep in front of the television. It was Jackson who saw him in the crack of the doorway, who grabbed his arm and dragged him in.

"Why are you naked?" James asked.

"Because it's hot," Jackson tested, and it seemed for a minute that James would believe it, before he drank in the particular pink of our cheeks and guilt in our eyes and catch in our breaths. Before he got to the "o" of Mom, Jackson's hand was over his mouth and he'd wrestled his little brother to the floor, made him promise not to tell. James was crying, and it occurred to me later it was not for the threat or the physical force, but because he had just witnessed something private, that he wasn't a part of: he felt, for maybe the first time in his life, alone. Like tourists tracing their fingers over the maps of the underground trains, wondering at how vehicles of the same origin so quickly split into branching.

We did not continue our experiments, nor did we mention them. But in the bath, beneath the bubbles, I touched myself and tried in vain not to feel my fingers, tried to understand why it was so different when someone else did it. I rubbed my crotch back and forth on the monkey bars at the park down the street, and though the metal was foreign, it was not the same as someone else's flesh.

(When I brought it up years later, Jackson denied its truth, looked at me the way people might look at an academic who has written a lengthy book on a subject so pigeonholed, so inaccessible, that the time and research involved seem at once pathetic and awe-inspiring in how unfathomable the reality. A memory so fierce as mine leaves one lonely.)

When my father caught me masturbating under the dinner table, he was gentle: he explained that it was perfectly normal but meant for private settings. When I grew up, it would be something very special to share with someone else. Nonetheless, my face grew red and I cried from shame. Later in my bedroom, I rubbed myself hard and wished determinedly for the time when someone else would be present for this warmth, this friction. And I knew, even then, whom that someone would be.

The secret, shameful feeling about sex that I've grown to have, which it's now clear Jackson long suffered, grows as I go farther back in eidetic memory, deeper in roots. It's been a part of my life longer than it seems it should have, which did not occur to me as good or bad until the latter lit up in bright lights—the type that shine through symbolical windows and keep one from sleeping.

Our childhood was a love affair like any other. Were I to choose my details wisely, I could submit them in present tense to a romantic advice column. We went through ups and downs, lapses in communication, periods of feverish adoration, epochs of lasting alienation. During the week he was gone one summer, I hung my quite long hair over the edge of the stone wall on our porch as if in protest, awaiting his return. Surely the act was in some ways Rapunzel-inspired but also a demonstration of the similarities between human relationships and the skin that hangs around our faces though long dead. Because yet they are dead or at best dying, strands of hair are worshipped and brushed and in some idyllic cases gathered in blue or yellow ribbons. Long hair is at best respected and at worst wondered at in the way old, strange things are: it is proof. It is history. And in the time of children, which is punctuated oddly and cataloged eccentrically, a week without Jackson was no less than a crater. What needs not be said, of course, is that the longer hair gets, the harder it is to brush.

Seen through another lens, the image of a little girl, craning her neck and spilling her hair toward her father's meager garden a few feet below, declaring that she misses her best friend, a little boy from down the street she's grown up with, is sweet. People like to be reminded of the child's pure compassion. It's this fierce, often pathetic mourning of love so innocent, which for good reason cannot exist in adulthood, that drives people to buy those posters of two six-year-olds pursing their lips on a beach about to kiss, or sharing the sound of the ocean coming from a seashell.

Shortly before his tenth birthday, James broke his hand on the oak tree that devastated the sidewalk outside my house. I stood with my legs planted firmly, hands slicing the air decisively, instructing him on how to throw a perfect punch at the bare bark. James's mother couldn't believe her son had been convinced, as my right hand had been wrapped in pink plaster for two weeks at that point. My father had been my instructor, had duct-taped a throw pillow to the tree, not thinking any ten-and-a-half-year-old's first attempt would make any serious contact.

I'd been physically pained but enthralled with my new-found power. I fell asleep in my new cast, fingering the ER bracelet, while my father cried down the hallway and thought of what he might say to my mother, to the woman who had birthed such a good punch. He thought he might apologize for his stupidity. He thought, or knew, that she would find it all hilarious. She'd call him an idiot and go to fix two more drinks, but the fifth would be gone, so she'd walk to the corner store and take so long returning that he'd begin to worry, but she would just be making small talk with the quiet-smiling Korean couple who owned the convenience store down the street. She would come back with a noisy paper bag and some little joke present for him: Jesus-scented incense, extra-large condoms in ludicrous gold wrappers. Then they would fuck in their immaculately white bedroom until the sun peeked in the curtains, her mouth open and smiling the whole time. When it was over, she'd tell him oh honey, oh lamb, this life.

But sex with the dead is always unsatisfying, and even after his forcedly enthusiastic efforts in masturbation, even when he tried to think of the elegantly weary and olive-skinned mother of the brothers down the street, his testicles were left as aching and sad as the rest of him.

O ur teenage years are just as engraved as the rest in my memory, but they are stories I am hesitant to speak about with anyone who wasn't present: because they seem boastful, fantastic, no doubt exaggerated; because in telling them we seem to lose credibility as the responsible adults we tell ourselves and the world that we are now.

The river, which we sometimes named as the catalyst for all of it, wasn't really a river. It was as an estuary, which is a fancy name for slough; it was referred to as a creek until 1959, when the town rallied for some national official or another to give it license as a river. Our parents were fine with calling it that, despite nothing about it being fresh or hurried, and just as accepting of what it spawned: walking bridges dotted with tiny lights, waterside restaurants that didn't charge for the newspaper and where people spent whole mornings sitting, antique store after antique store.

Separating the cafés where they sat with us on their knees, adjusting their sunglasses as we squirmed, was the corpse of a railroad that hadn't run since the town reigned as the egg capital of the world and every family had at least three chickens. Once we were old enough to walk, we tip-toed the steel lines in proud demonstration of newfound balance and secretly, gleefully hoped a train might still be coming. The rails are fenced off now, the wood more de-composed than not, and any drunk from one of the many nearby bars who is foolish enough to adventure onto them will most likely punch a foot through the sweet rot and fall fifteen feet into the filthy, barely moving water.

It's just one murky winding euphemism, really. Every-one who lives there calls it the river as if in the summer there are lemonade stands, beach towels, the smell of sun-screen, lobster-colored children, young mothers leafing through magazines. The wood of the docks decays slowly as the shopping carts sink into the silt and grime beneath the surface, groaning occasionally and remorsefully to the carcasses of fish and forty-ounces.

When the tide was low in early March, it became harder to romanticize. The tourists on the cobblestone promenade above turned their heads and clapped politely for the bland jazz bands. Below them, we remained loyal and observed the secrets revealed among the hills of silt: parking cones whose bright orange urgency had faded, lifeless ducks facedown, tennis shoes whose brands were unrecognizable or forgotten, Grocery Outlet shopping bags. We named our haunts along the river or accepted those that had been passed down: K-Dock, Lundry's Landing, The Woodbridge, Anus Beach, The Cop Shop.

Some meanings were forgotten; no one knew what the K stood for. Anus beach had once been Anise Beach, for the herb that grew there persistently. As for Bill Lundry, he'd fallen off the Woodbridge onto the putrid sand below; rumor has it that he finished his beer as he lay there half broken, that he would have died were it not for his sky-high blood alcohol concentration. I remember, still, the miniature jellyfish who returned from their travels once a summer for a month, briefly illuminating the river with undulating circles.

Different people like to tell different stories about the river, about the steamboats that held lavish parties during Prohibition or the people who'd occasionally drowned in it. There was a worn redheaded man who sold pot out of his backpack who liked to say that it used to be different: clear and green like a Rolling Rock bottle, and sometimes kids would even swim in there. I was happy to believe it, and believing can feel dangerously close to knowing.

When I got to college and my peers shared their adolescent experiences, I was shocked. They got into movies for half price on Fridays because Alex or John so-and-so worked there; they had their first drinks before or after prom and became too violently ill to really enjoy themselves; their Midwestern social lives were restricted by distance and whether or not a car was available; their curfews were strictly enforced; they'd had at the most two awkward, unfortunate sexual experiences before leaving home; their parents were bankers or involved in insurance and had done everything they could to provide a normal, safe upbringing.

A normal, safe upbringing was what our parents had (at least told themselves they) wanted for us, but the place we were raised seemed, the more we looked, to lend itself in every way to an experience that was anything but.

Among ourselves we've tried, cautiously, to dissect it. The pedestrian nature of the town certainly had something to do with it: everything could be walked to (though even the few spots that seemed unfeasibly far, we still ventured to), and the centrality made it such that it was easy to feign a respectable bedtime for a school night and slip out a window an hour later. Rarely did we associate indoors; our town was overflowing with unenclosed physical spaces just hidden enough and begging to be occupied.

Below the steel bridge that bisected the town into east and west was a three-by-ten-foot grated platform reached by ladder, and as long as our descent was discreet, no one would suspect that beneath the passing of cars was a group of laughing teenagers dangling their legs, feeling the rumbling, passing a bottle of cheap whiskey in the dark. The roofs of the old buildings could be reached by climbing pipes and fire escapes, and once atop one, other rooftop landscapes were easily accessible. An old Victorian that had been converted to an office boasted an unfenced backyard thick with sound-muffling redwoods and a wooden back porch to sit on; an alley on either side offered a high probability of escape in the case of police.

The roof of the old mill (which housed hair salons, a gym, clothing stores for middle aged woman that sold shapeless hemp dresses and wooden jewelry, and a wine bar that always seemed to be hiring) was a triumphant discovery: a series of intricate angles and slopes that provided secrecy and a clear view of both the river and downtown. I shared it only with Jackson, and it was there that finally we touched each other for the first time since the fall I was seven. (Later, as revenge for breaking his heart the first of a few times, he brought a whole host of people up there. They were too loud, the cops were called, and for insurance reasons they were carried down one by one in a cherry picker. My father happened to drive by and witness Jackson's abashed descent and declared it one of the funniest things he'd ever seen.)

They are fenced off now, only available to yacht owners who know the keypad's code, but the docks then felt placed there for our purposes alone. We sat on them night after night, physically below the town though feeling above it, laughing and separating from the circle to walk a few feet and pee off the side into the river. When the tide was especially high they wobbled in mimicry of our intoxicated states.

Bizarrely, the post office doors were always open, perhaps for the P.O. Boxers, though we never saw any, and so the post office was ours, too, though the echo of our voices across the marble floor and the tall ceiling was just not as friendly as across the river or the rooftops, and we reserved it for quiet end-of-the-night beers or refuge from the rain.

On visits home I am sometimes dolorous at the sights of these places, or the spaces they used to occupy. The large railroad trestle we called The Woodbridge was taken down almost five years ago in the name of flood control, though probably the real reason was that it had been confirmed that a dead kid found floating in the river had begun his night drinking there. Barbed-wire fences have sprung up around many of the places we entered and exited freely, and the narrow, thickly leaved sloping alleys named Pepper School and Telephone, which once seemed forgotten, are now brightly lit and trimmed of excess foliage.

It's not that I'd like to bring a brown bag of off-sale whiskey bought from the Central Club down to the docks and pretend that years haven't passed. It's that the lack of evidence makes the years spent distributing our weight in these places seem moot, makes it clear that our coming of age *was* improbable, that it *shouldn't* have happened.

The hiss of my father's oxygen tank punctuates our phone calls. His having to stop and force air through his lips every twenty seconds makes everything he says important, waited for. It always takes at least three or four rings for him to get to the phone; often he will pick up after I've begun leaving a message. He still has an actual answering machine, and I feel grateful in those times he is out to imagine my voice bouncing off the walls of the living room or perking the ears of the cat, who is unbelievably old and drooling at this point.

My father calls me dear heart even when he is frustrated with me. The fact that Jackson still calls him but not me is painful, and I can't bear to think of my father pressing Play and smiling while my ex-lover tells jokes or anecdotes into the answering machine. The fact that my father still loves him feels like betrayal.

I do not ask, but he reports that Jackson is doing phenomenally well; the abrupt disappearance of his problem has turned out not to be a fluke, although fingers still crossed on the part of Jackson and Shannon. While my father must, must know the sort of reaction even hearing the woman's name might elicit, it is unclear whether he believes there will be some sort of a therapeutic value or, having long ago accepted Jackson and James as a part of the family, feels the need to remind me that this is still the case.

She is a schoolteacher with apparently quite the gift for children; she is Midwestern with a rather pleasant phone voice and a warm laugh; she seems, according to my father, to be just the support system J needs in a time like this. He calls him "J." I can't remember him ever calling him "J" before.

My heart quickens and toes curl, but I stay quiet and do not ask my father to stop speaking of her. Instead my mind wanders and I think of the face that Jackson would make upon waking and surveying the damage he had caused or was still in the middle of causing: to find me up against the headboard, both my wrists pinned by his one, all of our bedding thrown to the floor and little pieces of down illuminated by the early morning coming through the window. His forehead crumpled from alien rage to bewilderment and desperation; he looked at me with disgust and pity, searching my face for a sign of guilt or fault. He had then, of course, turned away in shame and said nothing while I rose and showered and began to clean.

A coincidence, the fact that it has ceased since Us, is what those close to me have gently suggested out of obligation, but I remember that look. Though he wouldn't come out and say it, Jackson believed I had something to do with it, because why else would I go on forgiving him?

At the height of his teenage fling with speed, James spent a great deal of time with this guy who could do the *New York Times* crossword puzzle in under ten minutes. He (James) could make vivid sense of his math homework (and mine, though I was a class ahead)—he had not just memorized the theorems but could *apply* them, as we'd so often been urged to do, and did so fiercely. The mental image that burns for me here is of James in a well-worn T-shirt in the middle of winter on my front porch, trying to whisper so as not to wake my father but failing miserably, sweating and gesticulating with both a need and the self-imposed authority to explain. He began writing songs that were both catchy and disturbing, often with Dillon, the crossword guy, who was also into speed and had been a good five years.

While Jackson and I waited for an explosion of some sort, James coasted on his high with a no-matter-is-created-or-destroyed-type efficiency. He got a job as the graveyard shift desk clerk at a cheap motel chain way across town, which he took joy in walking to. He was always clad in secondhand suits and wingtips eerily reminiscent of his father's, and embodied that brand of extremely clean speed freak: hair always combed, no stubble whatsoever, hands raw from washing with the bar of soap he kept wrapped in wax paper in his pocket. He chain-smoked but also kept mints and cologne and tiny bottles of mouthwash in ready supply. His alert demeanor was perfect for the hours and even more perfect for the clientele: the drug addicts, the plain old homeless or near-homeless alcoholics, the crazy, the sad, the longtime alone—as a general rule, they all responded to James with submission and a vague assimilation of respect. If they attempted the usual hijinks, hot checks or soap theft or prostitution from their rooms, they forfeited almost immediately once he appeared at their door and bared his canine teeth grin offering a cigarette and a heart-to-heart. He spotted them stamps to send their insane letters, gave them more than two free refills of coffee; it was well known that if they wanted to wander in at four or six a.m. and sit in the little plastic lobby chairs while he composed his songs and talk or not talk, that was just fine with him. He was king of that place, and was after two months promoted to assistant manager.

With an obsequious shrug we accepted what the drugs made him and spent the night in the motel rooms he snuck us into. When it was just Jackson and me, we watched cable, passing the plastic ashtrays both listlessly and with an air of luxury, and later did what our parents would call making love but what we were still trying to figure out the nomenclature for. Some nights it was a whole group of us, and we did just the things you'd expect teenagers with free rein in a fourteen-by-twelve room all night to do. James would come in for ten minutes every once in a while, or however long it took to drink a beer; phone calls to and from the front desk just for the sake of a joke or were common and didn't lose their charm. We demanded three more pillows, six towels, a plate of gilded duck and in a hurry. The hours slipped by until we had to stumble out into the early morning onto the concrete balcony and make our way, reluctantly, back home.

To feel the person I loved most thrashing beside me, to wish I could intercept the antagonists of his nightmares, led to such feelings of powerlessness that at first I accepted the way he reached for me as an honor or at least a duty; I was glad that even in the depths of his unconscious, he knew I was there. He would kick so hard the bed shook, rip the blankets and sheets from his limbs like they were leeches, encircle his arms around me and work his fingers into my flesh so intricately it was as if he was trying to reach my bones. Deep in my rib cage, the small of my back, the curve of my shoulder. The first time I bruised, he was horrified, but I skirted the issue with dark humor—*Oh, honey, I know you only hurt me to teach me a lesson*—or lessened the blow by identifying shapes, as if we were cloud watching. A purple that bloomed not unlike a cactus, another whose abstract likeness suggested a fish. He felt awful but I assured him I placed no blame, that I'd never fault him for holding me too hard. At least you're not out smashing up buildings, I said. If the worst damage is a few points of soreness on my body, I'll wear them like badges. He kissed my forehead before we fell asleep each night. "Apologies in advance," he murmured darkly. Generally, our city wavered above or below a foggy sixty degrees all year long, and so the marks on my person rarely showed themselves. Jackson took to kissing them, somberly, slowly, and I petted the hair on his head and continued to forgive him.

There was no couch to sleep on in the San Francisco railroad flat we moved into shortly after college, but even if there had been, I doubt I would have retreated there or requested he do so: we'd shared everything since the beginning, and I couldn't see how his nightmares weren't mine. The children I nannied saw evidence of the bruises once in a while and wanted to know, like those their age always do, why, why, why. *Accidents!* I'd say brightly, knowing how they loved that word, its all-encompassing forgiveness. You could break, drop, lose sight of anything: cry accident and the universe said okay, all right.

One evening, amid a relative stillness, he brought his knee up so swiftly that it made contact with my lip. I stood in the bathroom, negotiating the swelling and bleeding, watching myself in the mirror, searching for signs of age and finding them. When he woke and witnessed the irregularity of my mouth in the morning, he wept and turned away. Asked me, please, not to touch him.

Shortly after Jackson's twenty-fifth birthday, I began to hand him pieces of charcoal and large expanses of paper, glue, bits of tulle peculiar in color, string, broad-stroke paintbrushes. What followed were images so compelling that I could not help but put my palm to my mouth and tilt my head sideways and breathe a little quieter, out of respect. Skeletons of lovers slumped toward each other in embraces beneath the earth, almost part of the roots but not quite assimilated, their backs, you could tell, broken. Sad-looking monsters with jagged triangles of teeth, trying to hold the too delicate in their large claws: pretty little boxes ruined, birds dead or dying. All of it in lines make-no-mistake deliberate. Though there was a softness, it did not come from any hesitant or small movements on the part of the artist.

I had wished only for some other proof of the life that Jackson kept while he slept, evidence besides the destruction of our home, the bruises and scratches on my body, but it was an experiment he grew to resent me for. He did not wish to believe that all those lines and curves had come from him without his permission or trust; more so, he was uncomfortable with the fascination he felt, in the mornings, tracing his fingers over the routes of ink or paint, turning the pieces over as if expecting an explanation on the back. At first we experienced a certain joy in looking at them, together, his eyes bulging, a slow grin spreading on his face that allowed permission for mine, often him drumming his fingers down my spine in affection and knowledge.

But then he began pulling out the tools in the daytime, assuming that if he had created these glorious stretches of melancholy sea creatures and skeleton lovers and the like in his sleep, he could do so equally well at our kitchen table while the sun was still shining. It caused him great distress when he found that he couldn't even hold the instruments comfortably, no less summon whatever inspired him so while unconscious. Cheap reproductions ensued. The lines had no confidence, and what had been stunning and jagged only seemed sloppy. That which was dark but hopeful and lovely in its desperation for redemption manifested, in the daytime, as only malevolent and one-dimensional.

His face, then, at the table he'd lovingly sanded, trying to speak a language he didn't know, was unbearable. I could only imagine what it was to literally compete with yourself. Being with someone for so long—forever, practically, in our case—made witnessing an experience that private, unreachable by empathy, an elaborate act of torture.

After several weeks he gave up. He bought a large old trunk that locked and placed the pieces we'd hung inside it. He slept like I had never seen him sleep: no words gurgling through from his dreams, very little movement, breathing steady and predictable.

Rightfully so, I was holding my breath the whole time.

It wasn't that James was unattractive, that there weren't hordes of females attracted to his strange scent as the years went on and he grew into himself. For him, the mystery of the other sex's body, the rituals, the phone calls, the tittering, the compromise of one's intellect for a brief period spent naked and sweating and writhing—it seemed inefficient, inconvenient, secondary.

How he felt about what we did in the bed opposite him was never much discussed. We assumed he felt no choice but to stand witness to our strange bond, which had forever been his role, even if this new manifestation of it was more complicated and visceral, even if it meant turning over or smothering his ears with a pillow while I sighed and Jackson grunted.

When it began he was nearly fourteen; at that point he was still just strange, and not strange-enchanting. His limbs had grown in without his permission, and he walked around as if constantly trying to retract them, a look of focus and anguish on his face. He had a habit of twisting the hair near his right ear around his finger obsessively, so much so that the skin around it began to grow red; he bit the flesh around his fingernails until they bled and seemed entrenched in a privacy more disturbing than intriguing.

At first he kept deathly quiet, and I couldn't help but take the split second between Jackson's adolescent thrusts to wonder if James remembered the evening he found his brother and me, both of us still children, poking at each other's naked bodies. If he remembered what his face felt like pressed against the unclean carpet as Jackson held his arms down and told him never to tell.

Any guilt I felt about it I allowed myself to smother in the justifications of love. Jackson and I had found adulthood long before our peers, were learning to combine limbs in inventive manners our friends would take years to master, knew what it meant to know the smell of someone's perspiration so well one could nearly recreate it in memory. Even if Jackson denied it, I think he knew as well as I did that James was awake and listening—there was no sleep talking, none of the typical shifting, not even one squeak of his mattress to parallel the squeaking of ours. In the mornings on the way to school he was blank, just wrapped his hair around his fingers and let his strange limbs lead the way; when we parted ways at the junior high campus, he rarely said good-bye, and at the most gave us a smirk and a salute. Later I learned from my father, who'd learned from Julia, that he had been falling asleep in the majority of his classes.

We were young—too young to be having sex, especially too young to be having sex that meant anything, but we never thought it would have much effect on anyone besides us. We certainly didn't predict the influence it apparently had on James, who kept quiet for nearly a year, who didn't make a sound until he made a series of them: loud, unavoidable, terrifying sounds.

It was a Thursday. That is to say, the day before Friday, which is the day we all looked forward to the most and detested once it came upon us, the thick slow classroom hours, every task more demanding, every question, it seemed, in several parts. So Thursday evenings, especially in the neighborhood we grew up in, which was overflowing with children then—Thursday evenings you could taste something bitter and anxious. It doesn't go away with age, either, this frustration with not being able to fast-forward minutes or hours. James was a poor student even well rested; he was likely more in need of three o'clock Friday than Jackson or I. Finally, something in him gave way.

I noticed them first, the noises, but Jackson was too absorbed in the alleviation of his adolescent erection to place them as coming from any other source but me. We'd been sleeping together long enough to have fine-tuned our frenzy, but I still got the sense sometimes, with him on top of me, that he was far removed.

"You feel," James panted in perfect mimicry of the words I sometimes uttered to Jackson during sex, "so *good*," and proceeded to make little female moans, placing a grunt just like his brother's every now and then for good measure.

I pressed against Jackson to stop but he was close to climax and took it for pleasure. "Please," I said, and he kept going. It was only once he came, when the room was supposed to be silent and filled with the last half hour, that he heard James's noises and reached for the lamp on the bedside table by the fish tank.

His underwear was off and his dick pointed straight toward the ceiling, but he was looking right at his brother, and I knew he had been the whole time. As Jackson processed, James began to smile. I wrapped the blanket around me but it couldn't or wouldn't cover every angle. Jackson looked straight at his brother and told me to leave, but I remained on the bed, trying to make my body smaller and smaller still, and I saw as Jackson leaped across the room how his penis looked flaccid in midair, and how James began to laugh and didn't stop until Jackson's hands around his neck had grown tight, and learned how the sound when someone is trying to breathe while being choked is like gurgling, and how punches sound when they are delivered slowly with the last bit of energy, and that you cannot only see blood but also smell it.

Even then, even bloody, even panting, still younger, still not quite the owner of his body, James locked his gaze on Jackson and grinned. He had won.

While it caused one of several breaks in communication between the two of them, I sometimes wondered through my shame whether what James had done had been his very best answer. He hadn't the maturity to approach Jackson, hadn't the power to scare him into stopping. Years later, when I woke next to the wrong brother, I felt like asking: and did you wish, always, that I had chosen you?

James's answers are short, and I try to imagine where he is in his apartment, what sits on his coffee table, whether he and his neighbors are friendly. Trying to engage him in conversation is difficult, as he barely leaves the two-bedroom his inheritance covers. My father sends him fresh flowers once a week, through a local florist, and I have to wonder whether they're placed in vases or just accrue on a sad, cluttered table.

"Not well," he says.

"How not well?"

"I don't think you want to know."

I insist I do, insist that whatever it is, I'd like to sit in his cage with him a moment. Since being diagnosed with bipolar disorder and then suffering from ensuing hallucinations and delusions, his voice has not changed; I think I wish it had. Because the next thing he tells me is that he has been writing funeral arrangements and eulogies for people who are not dead. That they are, if he does say so himself, rather perfect. How many funerals had I been to, he asks, where the person was accurately represented?

"And do you . . . do you actually think they're dead," I ask, but don't wait for the answer.

"Because if not, maybe it's a useful exercise in, you know, honesty, the evaluation of those you care about, the qualities you both admire and take issue with—"

"Right," he says, with cold precision. "Except I do. Believe they're dead. It takes my shrink reminding me, and I only see him once a week."

There is that myth, of course, which for a long time I let soothe me: *crazy people don't know they're crazy.* So he couldn't be crazy, this boy I grew up with: profoundly sad, yes. A sad person whose intelligence fostered, in his illness, a duplicity—that somewhere, always, there was reason.

Because a stay in the hospital was expensive and never fixed anything, he has become skilled in the art of withholding from his therapist the catchphrases that signal suicide or harm to self. Learned to bathe his face in wistful optimism and indulge the doctor's discussions of goals and hopes.

His first attempt was toward the end of Jackson and me; even now, I can't tell whether it kept us together longer or brought speed and velocity to our close. Julia had moved to Mexico by then. She'd completed a medical interpreting/translating course and was living the good life with a crowd of expats she referred to by affectionate nicknames over the phone. When Jackson had finally gotten hold of her with the news, she hadn't had much to say except that did he know that in Spanish, one didn't get "the blues"— you got "the purples"! Could he believe it? It was no use

with her, he said after he hung up. When he formed state-
ments like that, I wasn't allowed to agree or disagree.

We rose late the morning we were to visit him and were
forced to shower together. It was a tiny shower, but we were
experts in the geometry of not touching by then, switching
in and out of the water with precision, handing off shampoo
and soap without prompt. The smell and tingle of the tea tree
shampoo on my scalp and neck was close to burning, reminiscent of good, painful things. He finished before I did,
and I let the water run over me for a minute and wondered
if, from above, this looked like tenderness. Like intimacy.

In the common room where the nurse led us, the only
thing that clearly distinguished the patients from the concerned loved ones were the VISITOR stickers on our chests.
James wore slip-on canvas sneakers and a bulky tan car-
digan with leather elbow patches. When we asked how he
was, he shrugged like *Isn't it obvious?* On the phone he had
mentioned he was finding it impossible to read anything,
so we had brought him a book of crossword puzzles. He
scowled and said thanks, and I knew immediately it had
been a bad choice, an insult even. Crosswords were for
people with jobs, who wanted a chance to play in their
brain on Sundays over coffee. All he had been doing, I saw
now, was playing in his brain: dark, menacing, circuitous
games, with no rules and no way to win.

I was the only one who talked. Jackson was reserved,
suspicious. It seemed to me that he resented the pain
James was in: it came in daylight, its victim had acute

knowledge of the disease's spreading. The other patients I saw were likewise sedated, besides a chatty English guy with no visitors who made it his business to approach other people's. The couches were clean and newish, and the thin blue paint on the walls could even be considered pleasant. From somewhere in the rear of the hospital there was yelling that gave into moaning and then yelling again. When it grasped at words, it was in Spanish. We didn't ask, but James told us anyway.

"Carlos," he said. "Schizophrenic, I think. Has this stuffed rabbit he carries around. The one nurse truly fluent in Spanish is on leave for two weeks, can you believe that?"

The compassion in his voice made me hopeful, but his eyes darkened and he looked directly at Jackson for the first time.

"If only Mom was here, huh? Señora Bailey to the rescue." And he began to cackle until tears came to his eyes. The nurse across the room moved from where she was crouching, speaking softly to a near catatonic young woman in braided pigtails, and surveyed the three of us for signs of alarm. Jackson was not laughing. He sat with his arms slack, palms up, as if waiting to receive or accept some understanding.

The screaming in Spanish had ceased and I had not noticed.

"Woo," breathed James. "I haven't laughed that hard since—"

It was a sentence he couldn't finish.

While Jackson was the older brother, it often seemed otherwise in the eyes of our peers. He was an inch taller than James but never interrupted people while they spoke, never walked ahead or declared himself, in silent ways that add up, a king. He drank just as much as the rest of us (which was too much) but rarely appeared as intoxicated and was most likely to help someone vomit or listen patiently to maudlin rants. He read voraciously. He was drawn to fiction, as I was, but just as equally to fact. He read a biography of Jacques Cousteau with a pen in his hand, occasionally taking notes. For several weeks I fell asleep with his hand on my waist, him staring at the ceiling and telling me about Nikola Tesla. He could explain the magic of science so well that, in my mind, they were as good as his inventions, and I took pleasure in all the proliferating ways I'd loved him since childhood. Our parents, by then, had given up any weak protest to us sleeping together, and figured, somewhat correctly, that we took care of each other. It was mostly Jackson taking care of me, and me taking care of him by needing him.

Jackson had not told Julia about her younger son's relationship with speed: partially out of a loyalty stemming from childhood, partially because she probably wouldn't know how to deal with it any better than we could. He had dropped out of high school that fall, in his junior year, earned his GED, and bizarrely aced a few classes at the junior college (German, philosophy, marine biology) as well as assistant-managing the motel and writing music that grew consistently, and almost scarily, impressive. "Oh please tie a red balloon around my neck / the ribbon so long and the circle so full," he sang from the back of his throat in a song that haunts me, "so if I can't stay you'll see me through the depths / the living so long and the breathing so dull." The classes at the JC, he made clear, were not toward any sort of goal. They were for the sake of knowing—goddamn it—like they should be.

The explosion we'd been expecting came the summer before we were to leave for college, but not from the direction we'd expected.

James stopped around twelve, the age most sleepwalkers generally do. Jackson persisted. It generally manifested in the benign and comical ways everyone thinks of: he would walk halfway to school before waking up and realizing it was Saturday; he would fill the fish tank with silverware; he would pick up the phone and mumble into it, then leave it hanging from its cradle so that in the morning the operator was still crooning *If you'd like to make a call, please hang up and dial again.* So what happened, five months prior to Jackson's and my leaving our hometown, was a shock—though it portended the life he and I would live years later.

I had taken up with Dillon, the much older speed freak James was so fond of, mistaking his hummingbird mind for brilliance rather than years of drug use. I hadn't offered Jackson any real explanation or apology, just made small shifts in my attitude and ceased picking up his phone calls.

The rumors about Dillon were that he stole, he back-stabbed, he had once lit a tree in front of his house on fire and cackled while it burned until the cops came—but he took an interest in me, he wanted to talk about the books I was reading, began leaving strange packages on my door-step, calling the high school pretending to be my father and getting me out early so I could come down to the bar where he worked and surreptitiously drink for free. He was my first sexual experience besides Jackson, and it was com-pelling. In his strange apartment, he stayed between my legs until I could barely move; he shook and sweat and called me names I'd never been called; he held me so tight afterward I had to breathe a different way; he told me I had a mind beyond my years and that he loved me.

The affair lasted all of a month. It wasn't long before the exotic appeal wore off and I recognized him for what he was, which was downright scary, but it was during this time that James, sitting on the front porch on his night off, watched his brother exit their house fully asleep carrying a baseball bat that had been in the back of their closet for nearly four years.

The way James tells it, he had remained gentle the three blocks downtown, had tried to coax Jackson (whose fingers held the bat loosely as if it were merely an extension of his limp left arm) into turning around. But it was no dice, and so the younger brother followed the older brother dutifully, as he had so many times before. Given the considerable dis-tance that had grown between them during the period of his drug use—and more recently since I'd spurned Jackson and he'd grown even more solipsistic—James was glad to be alone with his brother, to do this small, quiet thing. The bat remained inert until, with a switch that seemed to affect Jackson's every muscle, it didn't.

All told, six windows were smashed and three cracked. When the cops arrived, Jackson was gone—how this happened, James can't explain or even remember. He had finally wrestled the polished wood out of his brother's hands, had stopped to catch his breath and shifted to find himself amid brilliant reds and blues encircling him where he stood with glass in his hair and blood on his hands from when he'd tried to intercept his sleeping brother's blows to the Shoe Repair window after restraint had proved impossible. Jackson must have wandered off as easily as he'd stepped out of bed and into the night, and no one, had they been awake to witness him walk by unhurried, would have suspected him of menace. They would have seen, instead, a young man with all the hopes in the world, bearing a gracious half-moon smile, up for a midnight stroll in the hometown he knew and loved.

James, on the other hand, was already a favorite of the cops by his association with Dillon, was bloody and holding a bat, had the telltale dilated pupils and high pulse, did not answer questions easily. He was searched, remnants of drugs were found in his pocket, blood was tested.

Given the town's quickly changing identity, or rather the fact that finally tourists had begun taking in its quaint values in hordes, there'd been a great deal of pressure from the city council to make an example of cases such as these, to assert that these sorts of incidents were not permissible, were not to be repeated. Both drugs and vandalism were on the rise, and as luck would have it, James's (Jackson's) crime included both. He had managed to crack in half the sign of the Shoe Repair shop, which was over one hundred years old (both the sign and the shop); he was charged with possession, vandalism, and defacement of a historic land-mark. Given his previous record (a minor in possession of alcohol as well as an evading arrest when we'd all run from the cops and gotten away but his pants had caught cartoonishly on a fence), it didn't look good for him.

As for Jackson, he found himself sore and vaguely satis-fied the next morning, as if in his dreams he'd swum hard and strong in a clear green river and his muscles had some-how experienced it. He began to feel uneasy as he rose into his usual Saturday morning routine of eggs-in-a-basket (he adored the concise circles like I did) and reading on the front porch. As the coffee began to take effect, he felt his body more clearly; the pleasant buzz in his lumbar region and the satisfied ache of well-used shoulder muscles sat outside the possibility of just a good dream. A smarting be-tween his thumb and forefinger revealed itself as a small, deeply lodged splinter. When he opened the screen door, he found that James's guitar was leaned against the rail-ing and his precious shoulder bag, which was never with-out him, was lumped next to it. He retreated inside to find Julia. Not because he particularly wanted to talk to her, but because the sight of her buried deep under the blankets, snoring, one arm extended straight out over the edge of the bed as if in greeting, or sitting up in bed staring at the wall remembering God knows what, was a signal of all things normal and familiar. Only she wasn't there.

A note on the kitchen table, which he hadn't noticed, read: YOUR BROTHER ARRESTED WILL CALL (The lack of punctuation and hurried scrawl made Jackson wonder, he told me later with a little laugh, whether his brother had been handcuffed and was waiting in front of a venue's ticket box, though that made little sense.)

It was at this point that Jackson buckled and broke the silence he'd instated toward me when I'd begun my affair with Dillon. For better or worse, this is usually the way these silences end: something awful happens, and the affected party returns to familiar comforts, temporarily forgetting the wrongs committed. My father let him in and he crawled into my bed and woke me with his crying.

What James did was stupid; what James did was brave. Perhaps he thought there was no way in hell they'd believe him if he said his sleepwalking brother had been the one swinging the bat, but more likely his silence was an act of sacrifice. Julia did not fund a lawyer, and though the public defender was a spunky, articulate man who was quick to point out James's steady and valued employment at the motel and his good grades at his one (and only) semester of junior college, the court found these red herrings and were more than willing to see him as a drug-addled youth whose potential did not excuse his actions.

Before his hearing, we went to visit him in the Juvenile Detention Center, where he'd walked into the visiting room looking somehow daunting in the dark blue heavy cloth jumpsuit, and he told us everything—the likes of which Jackson had suspected by the splinter in his hand, the soreness of his body, and the baseball mitt he'd found lodged inexplicably between his bed and the wall. Like blackout drunks, Jackson always had the feeling after one of his sleepwalking episodes that *something* had happened, only he didn't have drinking buddies to call up in a contrite state and question.

James took his usual time in storytelling: perfectly executed pauses, expertly placed details, hand gestures that shaped the air to his purposes. He even included that on Jackson's first swing he had tapped the bat on the ground once, as if heckling the pitcher. *Swing, batterbatter. Swing!* By the time he'd gotten to Jackson's remarkable vanish and the arrival of the police, the fifteen minutes were up, and so we couldn't ask him the question caught in our throats: *Well? Are you going to tell them?*

Jackson and I were to leave for college in the fall. We'd both been accepted at a small liberal arts school in the bland, ever-sunny southern part of the state, which had offered both of us a great deal of financial aid we'd have been foolish to turn down. A stay in jail, needless to say, would have put Jackson's plan for higher education on hold.

At his hearing, James was dignified and solemn. He smirked at us as he was led into the courtroom and sat up straight as he was questioned. When that famous question was asked of him, he ran his right hand over his still immaculately groomed hair and looked right at his brother.

Jackson's grip on my hand tightened so ferociously I winced and blinked in pain so that I heard, but did not see, "Guilty."

That three-second look, delivered with stolid, terrifying purpose, was to be the last communication between the brothers for almost seven years, until Jackson would accompany me into the lobby of an entirely different kind of institution where we carefully wrote our identities on sticky name tags and leafed through pamphlets about depression and suicide while we waited to be buzzed in to our James.

The hiss of my father's oxygen tank: I have not been listening for quite some time. Dear heart? He asks. I wish you two would talk, he tells me. You feel like you have a whole lifetime, but— He pauses. The hiss of his oxygen tank. My father has never stopped loving my mother, and I worry I may have inherited his capacity of never forgetting. Can it be called worrying when you already know?

After wandering away and back to each other so many times to the dark amusement of our parents and friends, Jackson and I finally called it even and settled our bets, began looking for an apartment that would house our history. We wandered through the vacant rooms holding hands like curious tourists, opened every door and stood rapt by every window. We had few requirements, felt shocked and grateful that any of these spaces would even accept us. We took the first apartment offered to us. The landlord, an aging hippie who seemed to wear all pieces of her wardrobe at once, rolled her eyes in near fondness when we kissed after committing our signatures.

We giggled with every discovery: two of the century-old doorknobs came loose with any turn slightly more than gentle; someone named Tobias had carved his name into the leftmost kitchen drawer; the shower supplied hot water for, almost infallibly, nine minutes and twenty seconds. In the days without furniture, we stretched out on the warped

hardwood and imagined the rest of our lives, later drinking whiskey in thick socks under Jackson's childhood quilt.

We tacked a map of San Francisco to the wall and consulted it daily, quizzing each other on bus routes and growing pleased at the way urbanity received us. We discovered
the concrete slides built for adult-sized bodies in the crests
of hilly affluent neighborhoods and flew down them on
the pieces of cardboard left behind; the bars you went to
when you wanted to be seen and when you wanted to hide;
the hotel with a pool under a glass ceiling that required
only finesse to sneak into. The little-known public roof
gardens in the financial district brought to life by a statute
dictating a certain ratio of public to private space: there,
we let our lives leak out over the robin's egg blue of the
oxidized copper that topped the oldest buildings, then the
sparkling bay beyond, and took comfort in the plentitude
of available air.

Julia helped pay for a foam mattress that adjusted to our
bodies and held our shapes gladly; my father donated my
mother's favorite coffee cup, a wooden dish rack, a coat
hanger made of found driftwood, and an outdated standing globe featuring nonexistent countries that spun at a
wobble. Jackson sewed three panels of curtains for the bay
windows around our bed, each four thick strips of muted
pastels: mauve, green, off-white, yellow. On the window-
sill, a terrarium of moss and succulents where plastic dino-
saurs loomed over tiny cowboys. On the nightstand, like
ever, a bowl of fish.

The peaceful sleeping after the imprisonment of his unconscious creations lasted two, two and a half weeks, and all the art pieces remained locked and quiet, though I half expected them to speak. He made it clear I was not to mention the landscapes he'd brought to life while sleeping, and I wanted to believe, along with him, that maybe their creation had finally quelled the thrashing he'd lived in struggle against for so long. While a few times I rose in the early morning to find Jackson not next to me, I found him only in the kitchen, making coffee; when he wasn't in the house, he was down the street buying donuts and fresh flowers. My careful awareness of his whereabouts made him angry; he wanted me to enjoy the baked goods and wide smiling sunflowers and believe, like he did, that it was over. In his mind, he hoped the art he'd produced in uneasy nearly dawn light was an expression that It had finally made what it wanted. And who could blame him, but it had stopped before, and there were still bruises on my body, faded and mottled purples and yellows.

And then, one morning, I woke cold. All the windows in our bedroom and kitchen were open, and our schizophrenic city had put the sun away somewhere and brought the fog back. A plate was set on the kitchen table; on the plate was a roll of toilet paper, our salt shaker, and a fistful of pennies from the jar we kept by the door. The door was open, and I dressed quickly. I was lucky this time and spotted Jackson half a block down crossing Mission, wearing his best suit and the hat I'd bought him at a joke shop; it sat slightly off balance and the little red plastic propeller lolled forward with the slight breeze. The balls of my feet were still agile, and they carried me through the mist just as a 49 pulled up and blocked my view of Jackson. The bus groaned as I approached it and Jackson floated up the stairs into it, gave the warm chuff of departure, its windows empty and smiling. I cursed and kept running, passing all things inert and defenseless—the Mexican market's fruit stands, covered in tarps, collecting dew, hiding lumpy secrets; homeless couples pressed together under blankets meant for children, their collection of precious garbage placed carefully around them; the sleeping skinless cat in the window of the always vacant odds-and-ends shop.

It took five blocks to reach the bus. The driver, an aging woman at the end of her shift, did not acknowledge me as I fumbled for my pass. PLEASE RESERVE THE FRONT SEATS FOR SENIORS, the bus warned, AND OTHER PERSONS WITH

DISABILITIES. He sat at the very back, his hands in his lap, the propeller on his hat moving with the air that came through the cracked window, a quiet, deranged smile fastened to him.

Had I sense or energy, I would have woken him or tried to redirect his course. But a shopping cart with a lazy wheel rarely cooperates, and there is something sweet in its commitment to annular wobbling. When the person you share a bed with snores or thieves the blankets or domineers the sleeping space, they are still the person you love. Jackson was still the person I loved, so I sat down and waited. The worst stretch of Market was beginning to wake: prostitutes cackling and playfully shoving each other outside single-residence occupancies, liquor store owners pushing the heavy rusted gates aside to unlock doors, the first of the train passengers descending underground, the hum of street sweepers. It was when I began to feel glad to be contained, carried, that he stood. The way he walked while sleeping was similar to the way children move while pretending to be soldiers: his knees lifted as if by strings, his back unnaturally straight as if a yardstick were concealed beneath his clothing, left-right-left-right-left.

I walked half a block behind him. The homeless men still in their sleeping bags smiled and cheered for him— "Diggin' that hat, brother." "Woo lordy you got places to be"—but as I passed they scowled. He was lopsided, determined, had every right to be there, and I obviously had none. However dangerous, the parallel tracks he ran on were fascinating, and in my weakest moments, which he came to despise me for, I didn't have the heart to intervene.

He stopped outside an art supply store and something tilted his head—another string—with the theatrical astonishment of silent movie actors, and I struggled to write the caption that would run across the bottom of the screen. It was barely six, but the store had just opened, for our city ran wild with art students and large canvas bags in constant need of refilling. I didn't follow him inside; I was ashamed to be there, ashamed not to have stopped him, ashamed to find amusement with this part of him that he so decried. Ten minutes later he was at the register, dumping materials in front of the clerk, who rolled his eyes and scanned them. Wonder of wonders, Jackson located his wallet and handed it across the counter: after thirty seconds of staring him down, the clerk shrugged, opened the wallet, and pulled out sufficient funds. We lived in a city full of crazy people, and this smiling man in a propeller hat and a suit buttoned incorrectly was not breaking any records.

He woke upon exiting the store, looked down at the bags in his hands clenched with a toddler's unyielding force, and dropped them when his fingers unconsciously slackened. A homeless man he'd passed earlier scuttled by, flashing a peace sign and grin of familiarity. In his wake Jackson saw me where I waited for him on the bench, my whole body tense. He joined me, leaned forward, put one hand on his knee and one, curiously, on his hat. He took it off, flicked the propeller grimly, and tossed it into traffic. When I reached to touch him, his body stiffened.

"I want to sleep so badly," he said. "To sleep and sleep and sleep, and to wake up in the same place, and have the world where I left it.

"I want," he continued, with his eyes closed as if imagining it, "to tell those boring stories about the dreams I've had to whoever will listen."

I cleared my throat with an air of solemnity. "I was your grandma but I wasn't your grandma, and you were in a house that was also a doctor's office?" I said.

"Yeah," he answered, "only time was like, something I could touch."

And we laughed and laughed until he kissed me hard on the mouth.

With his permission, I began to show his pieces to friends who stopped by our apartment, though I was careful to do so only when he wasn't home, and to put them back in the box where they stayed hidden. I needed to know that I wasn't imagining how perfectly lonely they were, how deftly they implied whole universes, simply because there was finally a symbol I could hold in my hand of my lover's other side.

Nathan, a friend of mine in grad school for philosophy, accepted my invitation eagerly as soon as I explained the situation. He was scary-smart, with a slightly broken nose that seemed even more broken when he smiled, and a tendency to overnod while listening. He chose words carefully, rarely swore, and seldom said a bad word about anyone.

"Jesus," he said and put his hand to his mouth just like I had done.

"Completely asleep?"

I nodded.

After looking at it a full two minutes, he removed the first from the pile and began to move through them quickly, as if he didn't know where to start, or that the next would surely clarify his feelings toward them. He paused and fixed on one I had a particularly hard time looking at.

It was mostly in charcoal, with some color added in pastel, as if saying *Go on. Smear me.* It depicted a nude woman with red strings of hair that trailed to her mid-thigh, head cocked and eyes closed in anguish; a hand was reaching out from her mouth, clutching a fistful of the hair that flowed down over her small, uneven breasts, the nipples of which pointed in different directions. The white of her too-thin torso was split open. Appearing grotesquely from her stomach was another hand, a leg kicking across the canvas at an odd, broken angle, and a male face smeared with blood. The face was round, bearded, smirking; the eyes looked straight ahead. The woman's feet were far too small and she seemed to teeter on the earth's surface.

Sometime after the last I'd looked at it, Jackson must have labeled it. In the bottom corner, in small milky black letters, it read: *I asked you nicely the first time.* I imagined him penning it, bitter and grinning darkly, desperate to assert authorship in some small way. Nathan put the pile next to him and clasped his hands in his lap.

"They—" He shook his head. "They have to be seen."

That night I phoned a friend who owned a small gallery. Though I had planned to seem neutral and merely curious as to whether he might have any interest, my words came across as imploring and desperate. My personal investment was obvious, and I shared too much about the effect the art was having on Jackson as well as myself. Paul listened as I blathered and did not interrupt. When I ran out of breath, he invited me over for dinner the following evening, probably more from concern for my well-being than interest in the pieces. I did not tell Jackson. Since childhood I had been using the eccentricities of his sleep in ways he hadn't authorized, but this, I hoped, would be different.

Dinner at Paul's was exquisite: pork chop with roasted peaches, sautéed green beans and mashed potatoes, a strong beer he had brewed himself. It was clear from my voice on the phone, he gently implied, that a large meal cooked with care would do me some good. While we ate he permitted me to speak wildly, about how incredulous Jackson and I had been when it first happened, how it continued even with all the materials hidden, the trip he made to the art store in his sleep. It was clear he was wary. Not of the validity of my story—he had a willingness to believe in the unusual that was endearing and familiar to me—but of art that was, well, *schticky*.

"It's maybe a poor comparison," he said, taking a sip of his beer, "but I'm reminded of that two-year-old who was recently lauded as an abstract expressionist prodigy. It was all over the place for a few months. The parents were both artists. They started giving her more than your average finger paint and printer paper. Canvasses, expensive oils and brushes, the works. And boom—through their connections they get her a show at a gallery, then another. The paintings started selling for ridiculous prices, and there were critics calling her Pollock reborn. And of course her success was propagated by all the controversy, whether her parents had helped or manipulated her, and then the big split between people who wanted to believe the paintings *were* real and *were* special, and those who called them phony. And before you knew it, it was more about the argument between the two groups, the believers calling the nonbelievers cynics, than the art itself."

Paul smiled bashfully and realized he had gotten lost in his excitement. He poured me more beer.

"And *then*," he continued more zealously, "that thing last year? With the elephants painting? Somewhere in Australia, I think. They gave the elephants paintbrushes and filmed it, and the footage cuts between the brush held in the snout and the canvas, and the end result is some real, like, thick Matisse-eque lines in a representation of an elephant. And what a sweet idea, I'll give 'em that, to think that an elephant would draw what he knew: other elephants. There's lots of evidence the footage is doctored, but people were willing to pay upward of twenty thousand dollars for an at best medio-cre painting, just because it may or not have been done by a zoo animal. Meanwhile artists with vast talent and sincerity are not getting anywhere, and often, more often than I'd like to believe, it's because they have no scheme. They're not tod-dlers or elephants, they don't, like, coauthor their work with an antique robot, they—"

He faltered and I smiled.

"Paul?" I asked. "Just look at them."

"All right, all right. But I promise nothing."

I brought the box to the table and placed it in front of him where he was propped up on his elbows, smiling wryly. I brought our dishes to the kitchen and washed them care-fully, letting the water run longer than necessary, feeling calmer than I had in a long time.

He was enraptured and didn't notice me come in. I placed a hand lightly on his shoulder and he jumped. I sat in the chair next to him and watched his face, which was glued to the pieces with consternation.

"Ida. Ida, I am so, so sorry. They're . . . they're nothing like what I expected. I don't know . . . I don't know what I expected, but not this. Not. This," and he waved his hand over the same piece Nathan had become stuck on.

"*'I asked you nicely the first time'*?! My God. So terrifying. And his *face!*" He stood and started moving.

"I'll show them. In a heartbeat. We've got to. The only thing is . . . him, right? He doesn't like them, is that right? Over the phone you said—"

"It's not quite that he doesn't like them. He just feels, I guess, that they don't belong to him, that he doesn't have any right to be congratulated for them. He can't, you know, do anything like them while he's awake." My throat caught, but he didn't notice.

"It's perfect," Paul exalted. "The best example of art that must . . . that there's just no choice about."

He was ecstatic and insisted I stay longer, refilling my glass of beer without asking and not noticing that my spirits did not lift with the warm carbonation. And why didn't they? I couldn't figure it out, quite. Wasn't this what I wanted, for an authority on the subject to be as moved as I was? The omission rang out: in Paul's praises of the pieces there was none of the struggle on my Jackson's face in the morning as he wondered at a secret part of him so gruesome. None of the pain of opening your eyes in a different place than you'd closed them, of feeling unsure of where you'd been and knowing you had changed the world in small ways. I left Paul's with the promise I would convince Jackson. I felt heavy with guilt and a familiar, obscure failure, like I had many years before when I'd tried to bring back what had been stolen and had instead unleashed forty-odd diseased, starving cats, clawing their way out of confinement, releasing a stench that drowned all else.

P aul's gallery space was small, with well-worn hardwood floors and no windows. Still, it had gained
respect in the concentric art world of our city, just as he
had with his brand of quiet, earnest charm. He was a trust
fund baby who lived modestly and took pleasure in fund-
ing projects and artists he felt to be noble. More often than
not, there was some kid from East Lansing, Michigan, or
Bentonville, Arkansas, or some other town you'd never
heard of, a talent Paul had somehow "discovered," staying
on his couch until he found his feet in the city. In being
so constantly generous, as well as having really quite the
eye for art others were likely to overlook, he had built a
following of people absolutely enamored with him and his
pursuits, no matter how ridiculous. Every opening he held
was full and buzzing with happy people, overflowing out
the door and onto the street, talking passionately about the
pieces inside, embracing individuals they'd just met. Jackson's, unfortunately, was no different.

He had grudgingly agreed to a show, though not without a great deal of resentment, and mostly to appease Paul, whose interest was endearing and had only grown with Jackson's aversion. After weeks of negotiation, Jackson had agreed to let his sleep's works be shown in the gallery but had no interest in an opening. Paul, determined, had pushed for a "quiet unveiling" late at night in loyalty to the art's conception; he promised there would be very little publicity and only modest curating that respected the artist's queasiness.

These promises, of course, did not hold up. For all Paul's munificence, he was still someone who generally got what he wanted from the world, and he had a hard time truncating his vision of desire. He made no posters or press releases, but his tongue was, as ever, free: word spread in the weeks preceding, and a substantial buzz began to sound.

Paul prepared furiously. He papered the ceiling of the space with pages of nineteenth-century French and German texts on sleepwalking and decided to name the exhibition after one of the titles, *Somnambulism and Cramp*, written by a man named Reichenbach who credited reports that sleepwalking was affected by the moon, and that sufferers were generally individuals with exaggerated sensory abilities; he called them "sensitives."

In the shortening days leading up to it, Jackson maintained he would not be present for the unveiling, which was to take place at three a.m. He grumbled around the apartment and took on the reorganization of our closets, the waxing of our floors, the oiling of our creaky dead bolt.

I caught him at the kitchen sink, sponge in hand and warm water running over his fingers into the empty sink, immobile and slightly smiling.

The morning of the event came, and we woke pleasantly. There had been no incidents the night before, save that Jackson had hopped into the shower asleep and gained consciousness with shaving cream covering his face and then decided it was time for a shave anyhow. The sun was shining, though the weather had predicted fog, and the birds outside did not sound like the kind that live in cities. He whispered me awake, tracing intricate patterns on the backs of my knees. He nibbled on my breasts as if he hadn't a thousand times before, he kissed me like he might discover something by doing so, he didn't let a strand of hair obscure my face, we fucked for almost an hour with our eyes open the whole time. And in the nature of lovers, we pretended, afterward, that it had been perfectly natural, congratulated each other on stamina and technique, did not mention that the last time our bodies had interacted in this way, the month was classified under a different season.

I scrambled eggs with fresh produce from the Mexican market, made too-strong coffee, and brought it back to him in bed. He had moved to lean against the headboard but his limbs remained loose in satisfied exhaustion.

He smiled dreamily at the bright primary colors of the food on the plate, then shifted his lightness toward me, and said, with wonder, "I think . . . I think I'd like to go!"

P aul's gallery was eight blocks from our place. The night was extremely warm, which happens in our city with no pattern, and at the most seven times a year. Jackson's mood was hard to navigate in that it was, just simply: pleasant. He smiled broadly at a weaving drunk making his way home from God knows where; he gave money to the one bum still out begging; he insisted on holding my hand; he had brought along a six-pack of a beer he used to love but that I hadn't seen him drink in at least two years. All of which made me nervous. Probably I had some idea of the evening's turnout, but only in the way that stiff joints often indicate bad weather though they can't accurately predict the how and when of the downpour.

I could hear it from a block away; it's funny how the amalgam of many quiet conversations actually feels louder (or rather, more emphatic) than human noise that is booming and frenzied. Of course, it was amplified by the juxtaposition of the hour: the bars had closed an hour before and the homeless people had put down their crime pulp paperbacks and flashlights and settled into their nests of scratchy blankets and cardboard. When we got closer, saw the cluster of people, Jackson stiffened with regret; his eyes began to take a terrible vacation. I knew, then, his coming had been a mistake.

The doors were locked. Paul was inside making last-minute preparations; I felt as though I could feel his mania through the papered glass windows and feared they would crack. He was listening to Leonard Cohen's *Songs From a Room*, the song "Seems So Long Ago, Nancy" humming through the glass and hovering above the heads of the crowd, the lyrics dolorous and apropos: "*In the hollow of the night / when you are cold and numb / you hear her talking freely then, / she's happy that you've come, / she's happy that you've come.*" The refrain lilted and retracted as my heart quickened, and I tried to estimate just how many people were there, how many I knew. When I sobered, Jackson had left my side and was making through the crowd with a quick pace that furthered my anxiety. He was aimed for the entrance, and purposefully, coldly touched people's elbows in the way that means *Let me through. Let me through right now.* Then he was knocking with increasing speed, the flat of his balled fist pounding rapidly. I couldn't see his face, but Paul's when he finally opened the door was an awful mirror. People were watching; whether they knew he was the artist was unclear, but it quickly turned the anticipatory murmur ominous, unsteady.

Through the crowd I saw James, knew instantly he'd been watching me the whole time. He arched his eyebrows not unkindly from where he stood on the outskirts. He was, as ever, strangely immaculate, and smoking his cigarette the odd way he always has, the filter held effortlessly between his middle and ring fingers. I was surprised he had heard about the show and more surprised that he'd come. The knots in my heart and chest reshaped themselves at the sight of my and Jackson's brother and my brain formed several dark rooms surrounding the possibilities of their interaction, given both the long and stubborn silence between them and the state Jackson was in.

I made my way toward him, our eyes locked and my feet carrying me without my explicit permission. Hi there, kid, he said or I think he said through my ears' insistent ringing. When he hugged me, I immediately let my body go limp, let myself focus for seven glorious seconds on not the impending doom but the way he smelled and has always smelled: like cedar and also fresh ground black pepper, like long loud nights and the ensuing regret, like history, like small but important reminders.

I, of course, needed to provide no explanations: he had seen Jackson's pounding at the door, had seen my face thereafter, had felt how gladly I'd received his embrace.

"Wanna hear a joke?" He smiled slightly, and I nodded and felt grateful for his ability to manipulate his emotional surroundings and those of others.

"So a guy walks into a bar," he said, already grinning, "and he stays there for the rest of my childhood."

I let it settle, then laughed to the point of hooting, all the frantic blood in my body happy for an emotional release of a different sort from the one currently pending. James was laughing too and we fed each other's joy, like only old friends who've been through much that is not funny can.

When the gallery finally opened, the people trickled in, all the more excited for the mysterious aggravated pounding of the man who, a girl who knew Jackson and me had revealed to the rest of the gaggle, was the artist. James entered by my side but took his cue and dissipated; my eyes found Jackson and I forgot instantly what had been so humorous minutes before. It seemed that Paul, if temporarily, had worked his magic. Jackson was, at the very least, still, but had arranged his body in a way that was a familiar, dangerous indication. He sat in the only chair in the room, one that no doubt Paul had scrambled to find in the hopes of placation. His left hand propped up his right elbow and his right arm crossed his body at a diagonal so that his beer rested on his left shoulder. It was an arrangement of limbs that simultaneously signaled inclusion, defense, fear, disgust.

Despite my overall queasiness and remorse, I recognized that the space looked gorgeous. The pages upon pages clinging to the walls were slightly shellacked and seemed to catch the light, then hold it. There was a modest assortment of strange items hanging from the ceiling on transparent cords: pieces of antique lace handkerchiefs, a faded pink rotary telephone, a rusted toy airplane (the left wing of which seemed to be half melted), several rings of skeleton keys, a mobile of a children's carousel of gilded horses, a few sepia-toned photographs, a chandelier at a ninety-degree angle, a wine bottle covered in different blues and yellows of candle wax. It spoke clearly to the obfuscation of dreams, to their ability to unite discordant objects into a string that is supposed to mean something. The floors painted a matte gray-black that still gleamed with few footsteps, and Jackson's pieces stretched and mounted as if they could ever be made uniform. Upon entering the gallery, the guests encountered a small block of text: a matter-of-fact narrative about how the pieces came to be and a biography of Jackson that was scant but made clear that he never, in his waking life, harbored artistic inclinations.

The people, who had been moments before factions of groups, became individuals, as is the result of all effective art. They put thumbs and forefingers to chins, they tilted their heads left and right, involuntary murmurs pushed out of their lips and rose. Paul stood at the back of the room, a few feet from Jackson's chair, his face oscillating between expressions of pleasure and agitation and a combination of both. Jackson was dark in a way I had seen only few times; he seemed to deflect light and noise. He was obviously not looking for me, but I found my body leading itself across the room, expertly maneuvering through the onlookers lost in their own memories as they gaped at the wondrous and terrible that had come to life while I slept. I saw myself stand behind his chair, saw my hand reach for his shoulder. Heard him say through his vacancy, without flinching, *"Don't."*

Paul's head snapped around as mine stayed still and unblinking, putting off processing what had just been said.

He looked from me to Jackson and realized, in the case of the latter, that there was nothing to see. The "artist" had retreated.

Unfortunately, the man in the seat, who looked very much like the person I shared a bed with, fit the bill in a way that further excited the people in the room. They looked from him to the art and back again, imagining the threads between the two. They were convinced that his stance and gaze were of someone taking it all in, though the truth was in every way the inverse. They wanted to assume they were important to him, that he was gathering their reactions to a large piece of his soul to reference later; they saw his posture as sweet, as a symbol of someone who is afraid to share but must. A few of them, after taking in each piece three and four times, began to gravitate to where he sat. Assuming sensitivity to his vulnerable position as a heart exposed, they crouched and spoke softly. They raved and paid respect and when he began to look at them but did not speak, they loved him further for it. He was, they thought, happy to let his art speak to them, viewed their perceptions as truth and felt no need to comment. The bold ones patted his arm and thanked him.

They began to trickle toward the exit, satisfied, once again becoming parts of groups, eager to discuss what they'd seen and felt. Jackson had only moved to reach for more beer, and once he'd drunk all six, filled a large cup then another with the red wine Paul had placed on the table for guests. Paul came over with a cocktail I hadn't asked for and gave my arm a squeeze. He let out the sigh he'd been holding in, and though I wanted to, I knew that this night would not be isolated. It would stretch many limbs out in just as many directions, and I'd be spending my every minute trying to chart them.

But then a woman I hadn't noticed made her way back inside. She was wearing a loose pale blue linen dress belted at the waist, flat leather boots. Her dirty brown hair was messily pinned and some strands escaped and fell down her cheeks, and she seemed determined. She could have been twenty-five or thirty-eight; her age seemed like something she chose day to day.

As she crossed the room Jackson locked menacing eyes with her, and my ears began ringing again, the water of my body revolted. She did not crouch to his level as the others had done, but stood and addressed him from a distance of five feet that seemed not to be for his comfort or security but hers. She revealed herself as a writer for the local arts journal, the sort that is free at newsstands but still respected and commonly found on coffee tables of those in the know. All of me flashed, and when I turned to Paul in anger, he had his hands in prayer position pressed to his lips. He tried to silently communicate that he had kept his promise, had not *directly* contacted the press, but I could tell a small, secret part of him was still pleased. It was then I cursed him as selfish, began to convince myself that he had manipulated me or brought all this about, instead of the reverse.

I expected Jackson to gaze just beyond her, as he had with all the rest who'd approached, but instead he made small adjustments that signified opening: he uncrossed his arms and set his drink on the floor, made Xs of his fingers and stretched them, inspected her and smiled, small and calm.

"Ida, Paul," he said, and actually changed his position in the chair, "Would you mind leaving Caroline and I alone for just a minute?"

And we did. We had no choice. Although the way he enunciated her name, with specious respect and cordiality, as if they were old friends with in-jokes, was terrifying. We had absolutely no reason to believe it would turn out well.

We stood outside together. The people had dissipated, but we could hear them making their leisurely, satisfied paths home, not far along and in no rush. The laughter and speech of educated people freed from a quiet space of intellect and reflection is instantly recognizable. It's a sound I generally cherish, a sound in which I find comfort and whole rooms of pleasant memories in my head, but that night it echoed in my ears as masturbatory and self-indulgent.

As children, we often stand by doors listening, but the doors are larger and the sounds we're searching for with our breaths held are of a different nature. They're news of an adult world we don't understand but wonder at the lexicon of, or perhaps the gurgle of a friend's teenaged sister on the telephone. In the first case we're probably hoping to hear what it is our parents are saying about the world we live in, and in the second we're enraptured with a world every source says we're bound for. Both occasions are somewhat joyous: as children, when we stand by doors, it is for a stolen pleasure.

Standing by a door listening as an adult always bears an ominous scent. It's always an act we know we should not morally commit but are driven by some grave circumstance to anyway. We are never absorbing precious bits of other worlds, but pieces of our own we're afraid to know but more afraid not to.

For the first minute, we heard close to nothing. Then Jackson's voice escalating, the breaking of glass, the thud and clatter of flat things reaching the ground.

"They're not mine," we heard, emphatic if muffled, then the female protest—

"THEY'RE"—crash—"NOT"—crash—"MINE."

We saw the doorknob jiggled and we parted in the arc of the opening door. Jackson, who strode into the middle of the street and made a sharp turn in the direction of our apartment. I allowed myself one peek into the gallery, where Caroline the journalist stood almost perfectly in the space's center with her arms wrapped around her torso, looking like an art piece herself, her face not blank but searching for an expression or waiting for someone to walk by and comment, fill her with their own memories and interpretations, then walk away and leave her bare again.

Following him home, twenty feet behind; his momentum was in every way forward and unapologetic. The few taxis still out not bothering to honk but yielding to him, the flashing crosswalks urging him on in solidarity, the bits of city debris skirting his feet as if curious. The door of our apartment not opening, something massive pushed against it. Still trying the key over and over, if only to feel that I was making something move and turn. Knocking first daintily, as if it weren't my home, then desperately, sliding down the doorframe and feeling the hum of the frantic beyond the wood.

I gave up after an hour or so and walked to Paul's, the sun coming up behind something of a cruel reminder of what had changed since it had been out last. The fuzz of wine and nervous breath hummed on my teeth, and the homeless people who glared at me from their cardboard nests suggested I was no better, like at least they had known when to settle.

Paul was not surprised when he answered the door. He smiled weakly and pointed his index finger at the cleft of his chin like, *Go ahead, I deserve it.* Instead I fell into him and he raised me like his new bride, placed me on the smaller of the two couches. On the coffee table was half a fifth of fine whiskey and on the other couch was Caroline, covered in a beige fleece throw blanket, her mouth open, one arm hanging off the couch, one sock on, all elegance and confidence and mystery gone. I reached for the bottle and drank deeply; Paul nodded in encouragement and gestured for me to pass it. We didn't speak, just drank and sighed, and I don't remember falling asleep, only gaining consciousness with the sounds of the park below Paul's window, the shrieks of children playing games. He and Caroline were both gone, and a note under the empty bottle detailed that there were strawberries and eggs in the refrigerator and that we should most certainly talk later if I felt strong enough.

Sundays in our neighborhood: brash, bright, infectious. Whole generations of Mexican families in their church best, the smallest children fussing with their shellacked hair, mariachi bands, orchid plants of every size and color at special prices, street sales, vendors pushing their jingling carts of coconut ice cream bars or churros or bacon-wrapped hot dogs. The smells and sounds Jackson and I delighted in waking up to, an alarm clock of life if there ever was one. I waded through them unnoticed and saw, upon reaching our building, that our bedroom window was open and the curtains in their simple ritual of floating in and out of it.

Jackson had removed whatever had been blocking the door, just as he'd removed himself. He had taken the things that he considered definitively his; some of them I hadn't even realized he recognized as clearly his until they were missing, and felt both guilty for not knowing and foolish for thinking they'd also been mine.

Our yellow cotton bedspread, on which I'd sewed a large patch of Jackson's childhood cowboy sheets, was now just yellow with a large interior rectangle of brighter yellow, some of the thread of the stitches still clinging. It would have been less of an insult if he'd just taken the whole thing, would have left me cold more physically.

What had he done with the fish? How could he possibly have taken all of them? Pictures formed in my head of Jackson distraught and carrying our fish in plastic bags, clutching them to his heart, asking then insisting people on the street move out of his way.

Some of the missing items seemed arbitrary. The bleach-stained bath mat, the antlers I'd found at a flea market and hung on our closet door as a coatrack. I wondered about where he'd gone but more so *how*. Had he stayed up all night frantically assembling what he considered his until the U-Haul office opened? It was possible, but the image in my head was that of a one-man band, limbs bent in odd ways to accommodate the various objects, already vestiges of our life together. How quickly other parties decide which is past.

W hat about the fish?" I demanded, like the answer
might reverse the past week. Like surely if I could
locate the fish and bring them home, Jackson would follow
out of default.

"Alive. Mostly."

"Mostly?"

"Right. Mostly," James said, already bored by the subject.

Eight days after the morning after, James called me on his
graveyard shift at the hotel in the city where he'd worked for
nearly half a decade, the place he'd graduated to given the
glowing recommendations from the seedy franchise motel
in our hometown. It was three thirty in the morning, and
though I was awake, I feigned a hypnagogic calm that indi-
cated I was still a normal, nondistraught human being who
crawled into bed at a regular hour and woke eager for the
day. Of course he probably didn't believe me, but pretended
for my sake. A large part of loving someone is knowing
when to pretend and when not to; "make-believe" is a game

children play but adults wrote the rules to. *Pretend,* Jackson would say while we whispered in the postbedtime dark, *pretend we're in the ocean and have to live our lives here. Pretend we've got to convince the sharks we're good. Pretend . . . pretend I've got a sword the king of the fishes gave me. Pretend you're scared.*

"How you doin'?" he said, and I regretted his dropping of the "g"; this was not a time for casual speech. I wanted hard consonants, harsh pronunciation. I wanted every word.

"I am . . . that's a good question." And I thought about it. "I'm just as you'd expect?"

James snorted. While what I wanted was a sigh or a cluck of the tongue or other subtle mark of sympathy, the snort required an honesty I appreciated.

"How are you?" I retorted meanly, but he didn't take the bait. I could tell by his breath that he was outside smoking, the cordless phone straining to connect the two of us, the cars on Lombard passing over the speed limit, still reeling from their stint on the freeway.

"Look, kiddo, I don't even want to tell you this, not supposed to . . . but . . . listen. He's fine, all right? He's, you know, respirating. And eating, sometimes. He's fine. But Ida, he doesn't want to talk to you, and I mean doesn't. He had me take his phone away on account of all your calls and—"

(On the other end, across the city, I was silent. The phone call, the mention of him, made all of it real, made the past week where I'd sat in our haunted apartment barely eating or showering and wearing exclusively a shirt and pair of boxer briefs he'd left behind, the result of an actual event and not just some error in communications.)

"And honestly, I wish you'd stop. Think you should. Look, it's not my place, or maybe it is—I've known both of you my whole life but Ida? What did you expect? How did you think he'd react?"

I interrupted him there although I knew I didn't, hadn't, wouldn't have any authority over the conversation. I had, in the last week, lost any power, and in a strange way it was freeing, in a sense it allowed for behavior previously barred. I was permitted icy single-word answers, listless-ness, the inability to listen.

"You know, it's funny," I lashed, "how you're suddenly a big piece of our common history again. After for years I had to tiptoe around mentioning our past. And kiddo? Don't call me kiddo. I was writing in cursive while you were still accidentally pissing yourself, pretty much." Which was a lie, and both of us knew that.

"Ida, just listen. It's the same. He's never appreciated having decisions made for him and I know . . . I know you guys have been together forever. I know it must *feel* like you're an extension of him and that you can, but you're not. And you can't."

"He's at your apartment, then."

"Right. Yes. But not for long, and I promised I wouldn't . . . don't come here, okay? I'm sorry for how you must be feeling. But I think he's probably right. What you did was—"

• • •

I didn't go there. Didn't much go anywhere. Conducted experiments in starvation and isolation. Paul called non-stop and baked and cooked and left feasts outside my door, which I stubbornly refused with the exception of the corn bread he dropped off on day three. He had wrapped it in a red-and-white-checkered linen cloth and tied a blue ribbon around it. It was a portion large enough for three, and still warm: I held it to my chest as if it were a child and lay on the couch with it and wished Jackson could see. It tasted perfect and made the whole room smell like fresh butter, but I'd waited too long to eat and attacked it like a savage; he hadn't used enough flour and it fell to pieces. Eating off the floor is oddly satisfying. Honest.

The piece Caroline wrote was minimal. It had been her, she'd explained to Paul, who'd pitched the piece, and so even after the whole episode she had no choice but to write it. The piece sat off center, dwarfed by the color photography and coverage of a lavish parade the previous weekend.

SOMNAMBULISM AND CRAMP
Original Art by Jackson Bailey

More than 50 people crammed into to Paul Flowers's studio on 24th and Hampshire for an art opening that began at 3 a.m. last Saturday, which no one promoted but everyone had heard about.

Curated deftly by Flowers with modest bits of cynical ephemera, *Somnambulism and Cramp* displayed the works of debut artist Jackson Bailey, whose close friends claim he makes art in his sleep.

The enraptured crowd stumbled in lacking any expectations and were slow to leave.

The pieces, reminiscent of dark fables or didactics for naughty children, remain unavailable for purchase.

The artist declined to comment, except to say, "They're not mine."

Below the article was a small black-and-white photograph of Jackson in the chair he'd loomed in the entire night, looking straight ahead, the *I asked you nicely the first time* piece on display behind him, and I knew, watching it as if waiting for it to move, what it must look like to everyone else. I saw a photograph of something private, an animal caught in its most intimate act, but I knew the photograph everyone else saw displayed a man with confidence and many years ahead of him. All my life, it had been he and I versus everyone else, but in his exit he'd made the equation convoluted. Us versus him versus me versus the rest versus him again. And while I have a mind for numbers, enjoy the construction and reconstruction, multiplication and simplification of variables, I couldn't have extricated any solution if I tried.

You *don't remember,* I used to say to him, first with semi-comic dramatic incredulity and an open mouth. *You don't remember,* quieter, the last couple syllables swallowed. The conversation grew in circles from his inability to recall, say, some punch line, a perfect afternoon some three years ago, the terrifying type of off-brand whiskey that we drank too much of and that allowed us to sleep together for the first time. The prompts pointed to something larger, of course, of the ever-present tightness in my throat born the moment my father explained the difference between shared blood and proximity. It might be safe to say that during all the years I spent hoping he needed me, I was simultaneously daring him to prove he didn't by citing his small failures in documentation, in reverence. While I didn't receive the traditional breakdown of reasons for leaving, didn't get the chance to stutter and beg, my knowledge of him easily produced his answers: *I can't so determinedly classify every moment as an investment in the future.*

Hopes are different than plans, and even careful plans rarely actualize themselves exactly according to the blueprint.

A false cognate that's always struck me: in French, "attendre" is not to attend but to wait. How different the structures of being there, present and participating, and waiting, how palpable the confusion between the two. I supposed I was expecting him to get somewhere. It's a form of waiting that's harmful, in that you're really not anticipating any external force but rather some clear and brash interior shift. And did he ever get somewhere, bubbling over in a way that altered the course of our lives, though it was a different kind of destination, a different kind of event, than I was hoping for. I had plans for him of therapeutic transcendence, the wish that he could feel like the gruesome things he'd done while nightmaring had at least added up to a whole he could look at, examine, maybe experience a sense of pride. Instead they pushed him in another direction, instead they asserted his suspicion that no matter how he measured himself, there was this other darkness that insisted on living (and loudly).

I'd hoped it'd be a gift. Hoped he would feel, at last, forgiveness, support. The sense that however much he writhed, it was to a point. And selfishly, perhaps, I wanted him to look around and see that I'd accepted his worst and loved it.

It hurts to replay those conversations and find evidence of his effort, recognize his keens as a love I named insufficient. Of course I remember, he would say. Just in a different way. I remember by never putting too many ice cubes in your drink, because your teeth are ultrasensitive to cold. I remember by watching where you put your keys and pointing them out to you later. I remember when it's early in the morning and I'm in the shower feeling the BB pellet you put in my back. I remember by watching you while you cross a room with the same stride you've always had, uneven and heavier on the right foot and bold. I remember by not having to explain myself. I remember. I remember. I remember.

Whether Jackson remained with James for days or weeks was never revealed to me. I only know that he stayed in his apartment and accepted kindnesses from the brother he'd barely spoken to—save the visit we made to him in the hospital, during which Jackson hardly opened his mouth—since we sat in a small room with no windows and James told us about the swings of the baseball bat, the sudden and encompassing swirl of blue and red lights. If they talked about the trial, Jackson's guilt/remorse/resentment, the science-fiction novels and bland ham sandwiches James devoured in jail, the years in between, the bruises Jackson's sleep left on my breasts and neck, neither chose to tell me.

Years and years and moments upon moments were suddenly negated. Since childhood I've spent my heart and words and a catalog of tiny, insignificant moments trying to merge with a bloodstream not mine. The achievements of assimilation many; the failures less often but grander in scale. My father had to take me aside when I was six and explain to me that while it might feel like it, honey, James and Jackson are *not* your brothers, and so it's no good to be running around calling them that. And I crawled into his lap and cried and choked and gasped until I couldn't, fingering the ivory buttons on his rough linen shirt and feeling, for the first time, the pain in trying to understand the word that should be simple: *family*. If not my brothers, then what, I asked? And he taught me another word that should be simple: *friends*.

And so while James brought Jackson food and books and the oatmeal soap he requested, I sat in the apartment my past bequeathed me and slowly began making the phone calls that other people dread answering. I swallowed my pride and a great deal of anti-anxiety medication Paul had brought, like everything else, without my asking.

These are the type of phone calls that everyone receives from time to time but that no one wants to admit making. They are to people one hasn't spoken to in a significant amount of time, and they involve self-centered apologies, circuitous anecdotes, the repetition of stock phrases "I don't know," "It's just that," "If only."

I had let myself forget: that honest-to-goodness, forever families are made of blood. That a history doesn't guarantee a future. That no matter how many secrets Jackson and I had told each other; no matter how many times we'd returned home to find the other waiting; no matter how many seasonal colds and flus we'd spread back and forth, taking turns playing nurse; no matter how many, no matter how much, he was not my family. And neither was James, who was happy to be reunited with Jackson and wonder sweetly at the common acids, pigmentations, and chromosomal intersections.

I called friends and feigned interest in catching up, but their good news made me resent them and their bad news paled in comparison to mine. Those who knew me more intimately let me cut to the chase, rehash the last three or five or twenty years of the relationship. And what I wanted was someone to simmer incredulously with me, to deny that all of this would last, but they always offered advice. I should take up jogging or tennis or, one suggested after I rejected everything else, perhaps smoking again, at least temporarily. The majority of conversations ended this way, but still I went on making the phone calls, "reaching out," using words and terms like *"profoundly sad"* and *"head space"* and *"grief"* and *"I wish he would just call and let me know where he is"* and a great deal of expletives.

"Fuck," I would say, after I'd exhausted the story for the fifth time that day. "Fuck!"

Besides friends I'd forgotten—who'd essentially forgotten about me—I called my father, who listened but would not commiserate.

"Dear heart," he said with a sigh, "I want you to hear what I'm about to say and try not to be angry.

"You and Jackson . . ." he said, and all I heard was the familiarity of our names once again united, ". . . you and Jackson have had your time. I'm an old man, and I know what I'm saying when I tell you that just because you love someone, Peaches, just because you love someone doesn't mean they're right. For you. At least not forever. And how many times, Ida—how many times have I picked up the phone to you in a state of absolute disrepair because you've woken up to him gone? How many times have you worn long sleeves in the summer—I don't care if it's not his fault he hurts you, Ida, but the truth is he does. And you hurt each other. You're my child and Jackson might as well be, and don't hate me for saying this, honey, but I think he was right to go."

When I had run out of old friends to call, and even my father said he'd be happy to talk with me about anything but Jackson, I began calling James's hotel. He was required to pick up and so I was able to get in a few angry words, hammer out a few reluctant answers, but after two weeks he convinced his boss of a frequent prank caller and the need of a little box that he glanced at, then ignored, while the telephone wires ached and the numbers of my location pulsed and pulsed and pulsed.

Amid all of this, my father and Julia undertook partnership wholeheartedly, almost as if it were their profession. They made an art form of consideration, compassion, frequently stumbling over each other to accommodate. Rolls of Tums showed up with the slightest mention of stomach upset, you-shouldn't-haves exchanged like currency. Whatever tension there'd been decades ago, as young parents trying to survive in different ways, they relegated this like an old couch for the sake of something more comfortable. She moved from the room where I had slept as a child to his. Though they slept in the same bed, we understood this was not for the sake of lust but nearness; Julia wanted to be there in the middle of the night if my father's breath grew troubled, and he felt obligated to receive whatever end-of-the-day or postdream thoughts she offered. In a word, Julia navigated all things physical and tangible for the both of them—trips to the post office and the pharmacy, groceries, whole days mopping and sweeping—and my father held her hand and listened, read her short stories by Latin American authors about little boys sailing and drowning in a sea of light.

There are photographs I could display, stories I could tell, that would mitigate harsh images like that of Jackson sitting demonic in the chair at Paul's gallery, of him looking down at the most recent bruises on my breasts and turning away, not able to manage the information. There were whole days laughably perfect, those we memorize to nourish us later. Of course, I try to reject turning to these for hydration, given the subsequent drought and its crater I sat in speechless, but it would be unfair to him and, mostly, all that time, to say we faltered for the entirety of it.

There is a game we used to play, after sex, in which we'd try to stay connected afterward for as long as possible. As in we'd lie there, adjusting our bodies and breathing patterns to avoid possible displacement, having conversations about the books we were reading, the man at the corner store whom we loved, our parents, the status of the tomato plant we tried raising several times. It's silly to describe, the next part even more so, but sometimes, on the heaterless winter mornings in our apartment, we'd try to get up like that, the comforter wrapped around both of us, my legs around his lower back, and he'd sometimes succeed at pouring a bowl of cereal that we'd then share, me still suspended and calves straining to grip, giggling but trying to refrain from doing so, wanting to be a part of the same warmth. We'd put our serious faces on again and he'd oscillate between an exhausted, happy still and an erection, and sometimes we'd enjoy each other again.

Were I testifying for a case of happiness, there's much else I'd mention. For instance, the fact that we never bought a mop, preferring instead that childish thing where you attach damp cloths to your feet and slide across the floor. A Sunday evening ritual, with beers in hand that sometimes dropped and made the cleaning all the more necessary. There was much of adulthood we had no idea how to navigate, and new challenges arose all the time, but we found ways to live happily within them, and the shrieks as we cantered down the long hardwood hallway were loud.

I might also tell the jury how talented we were at presents. My because-it's-Tuesday honey sticks countered with his fish of strange colors waiting to be named, my strings of little lamps made of mason jars complementing the cerulean he'd painted the living room as a surprise. I'd mention that he mostly always placed a glass of water and two Advil before me without my requesting it (he just knew), that he had a habit of buying fresh flowers and a knack for arranging them. That also a favorite joke between us was to tape a terrifying photo on the inside of the toilet seat or the cabinet, ideally at night so the other would find it in the morning: that famous mug shot of Nick Nolte, a particularly disturbing image of Carrot Top post steroids.

Everyone who visited our home found it just that. They clucked their tongues at the history it implied, some awed given their free lifestyles as just one person, some envious, some inquisitive. We hung photographs by wooden clothespins on a string that ran the length of the east wall. My father and Jackson, age nine, on the afternoon of the Fourth of July, Dad holding a fifty-dollar brick that Jackson is fixated on, fascinated by the promise of pyrotechnics. James and Jackson and myself, sitting on the steps of Julia's porch on what was my first day of high school. James has grown shadowed already, turning his face away from the camera so that his awkward nose seems larger, doing that thing boys of that age do where they hide their hands inside the sleeves of their sweatshirts. Jackson in a worn shirt that details species of birds, his eyes so bright they're almost garish. Me in a tight-fitting striped linen button-down that I adored and jeans I'd put holes in over the summer. There was evidence of later years also, of course. Jackson and me, home from college for Christmas, smoking cigarettes on someone's absent parents' back porch, in on a joke, our blooming intellectual freedoms nearly a third figure in the photograph, one itchy scarf wrapped around both our necks. Jackson pissing off the winding two-lane highway that follows the edge of California and sometimes closes for repairs when chunks fall into the ocean. A picture taken just after, the first morning of the camping trip we were driving toward, of our faces mashed against each other in the two sleeping bags whose zippers we tricked into meeting. James at sixteen with his guitar on Julia's porch, singing and his mouth open as if waiting for the unbridled refreshment of a hose, Jackson and me barely visible in the background, smirking at each other; my father's thumb in the bottom left corner, so intent on capture that he was careless.

When new friends came over and saw all of it, when they asked how long we'd been together, we had several answers.

"Since somewhere between simple addition," I'd start, "and multiplication tables," Jackson would finish.

"Since before cursive."

"Hell, probably since before we knew the alphabet."

Some of them wanted to know: And do you fight? And we would say: Yes. Of course. Doesn't every family?

P aul couldn't explain how it happened, but given the circumstances, it was the one blunder of the evening I forgave him for. Somewhere between Jackson's frenetic outburst at Caroline and her subsequent breakdown, *I asked you nicely the first time* went missing. Though we both remembered Jackson leaving the space empty-handed, we both figured he had something to do with it. It was too obvious a symbol. He had asked us nicely the first time, hadn't he? He had asked me not to provide him with the materials in his sleep. Not to let him take buses and wander into art stores. Not to show anyone, and certainly not to exhibit the pieces. He had asked nicely the first, second, and third times, but I had insisted, as always, on knowing that surely this would do some good and instead unleashed, once again, that which was diseased and clawing.

Three weeks later the piece appeared for sale on the Internet. Ridiculous, many-pronged threads ensued about

how Jackson was a hack or Jackson was the biggest talent to emerge in years or Jackson was rumored to abuse
women. A bidding war actualized, and the seller, whoever
it was, let it rise. Paul called and asked if I wanted to pursue
legal action, to find the thief, but I didn't respond. Jackson had brought about explosions on several fronts, and it
seemed only logical to me that there would be more.

What didn't seem natural was the money that appeared
in Paul's mailbox with a handwritten note in neat capitals
requesting he forward it to the artist. As Paul didn't have
any better idea of where Jackson had gone, I accepted it,
but only to spite Jackson, to prove to him that I'd been
right: what he did in his sleep, whether or not they were
"his," were gut-wrenching and compelling and other people loved them so fiercely they were willing to pay upward
of a thousand dollars. That someone would steal the piece
only to return the money would have to mean something
to him, I thought.

I begged and manipulated James for his brother's address. He refused and spoke in thick condescension.

"I really have to say here, Ida, I still agree with Jackson
that it's better if you two don't talk. I am sorry, but no. No
can do. Nope."

On my second try, he was just as short but slightly more
kind, had forgotten how much he was supposed to hate me
as per his brother's instructions, and I played it for everything it was worth.

"How you doing tonight, kid?" he asked, and I let him
call me kid; being the needy versus the needed was essential.

"Oh, you know," I said and composed a self-aware titter, "it goes up and down. But I'm trying to think of other things? And let myself feel but not *sit* in it?"

"That's good. That's real good."

"Yeah! And I even started a little garden on the fire escape today."

I was lying through my teeth. There was absolutely no happy-go-lucky gardening going on, no brightening at the thought of readily available fresh rosemary.

"All good things," he said.

I hedged my bets and let him talk about himself for a while, resolved to let it wait.

On the third try, I embarrassed even myself with insipid, upbeat blather that filled the telephone lines until they could barely stand it, and without taking a breath posed the question again. I used my very best manipulative lilt, stressed that he really could probably use the money, considering he was starting his life over, that this wasn't at all about making contact with him.

"You know," I posed, tried to imbue my voice with all the begrudged wisdom I could, "despite everything, I still care about him. He did what he felt he had to do."

It was an evil game I was playing, outsmarting James, taking advantage of someone who couldn't help but bow to our history. Despite years, despite so many divergences, I was still the older girl from down the street who held his head while he vomited after too many popsicles and so couldn't tell his mother he was ill, still the girl who slept in her underwear on the floor five feet from him for years after society deemed it permissible because I was, after all, essentially his sister. Still the owner of the first pair of breasts he ever saw in person, when Jackson and I broke into the high school pool and swam naked and kissed naked and did other things naked while James sat on the bleachers silent and sullen and clothed.

We were family, and though the person who mattered most was far away in another city and had forgotten, I had won. James agreed to give me his brother's address as long as I promised to send the check and only the check.

Jackson returned the check and I sent it back and he returned it and I sent it back and it went on for nearly a month. It felt nearly like flirting, the interval between its return becoming shorter and shorter until the fourth week, when I waited to spring with my supply of stamps and envelopes and it never came. It was supposed to feel like winning, but didn't, and though I'd searched each envelope he'd returned for any sign of him and never found anything, when they stopped appearing through the brass slot and falling onto the crooked floors that had been ours, I wished I had searched harder, was sure I had missed something. When my father called and I told him with a pathetic giggle of our exchange, he danced deftly around the topic.

The plus or minus sign is supposed to appear within two minutes, but on all three the former appeared immediately.

There was absolutely no question of "keeping it"—as if it were something found—but still, I mentally drew Punnett squares like in high school biology class, remembered that blue eyes like mine are a recessive trait, as is my widow's peak. The nausea not just in the mornings. The constant glances into mirrors and the windows of trains, begging they forgive my vanity, silently explaining it's not just me I'm looking at or for, that I should have paid for three tickets.

I wanted to tell everyone, wanted to tell no one. I saw pregnant women and wanted to say *I'm seven weeks*, wanted to glow with them and not disclose that seven would not turn to eight. The dreaminess, the pernicious hunger. My hand wandering onto my abdomen without my permission, every gesture an apology.

The day before the clinic I woke early, took half of Jackson to a museum and showed him—I was sure it was a him—my favorite Rauschenberg and stood there twenty minutes so that he would remember. I splurged on fine coffee, sparkling water from France, fresh-squeezed orange juice thick with pulp. The sun was out for the first time in weeks so we headed to a roof garden with a view of the water and I read poems and stories that I hoped would help him to understand what it is I was saving him from. At seven weeks, his lungs and liver and ears and mouth were being formed, and his heart, beating with one chamber, would soon have formed a dividing wall. Since his couldn't, I swore to form divisions in my own.

The terms they use at the clinic versus the ones they must use with happy couples at the regular doctor's: *I see the pregnancy*, said a nurse named Viv, not *I see the baby*. I asked to see and collapsed into sobs but still not letting her turn the screen away. Using the scratchy paper draped over my naked bottom half to wipe my face. I remembered hearing how abortion clinics in the Midwest are required to show the sonogram, that a significant number of children are born because of this.

Viv asked after my support system, which really meant: and what about the father?

"Oh, he's been great," I lied, shocked at myself. "We're both just real sad we can't keep it, but our financial situation—you know."

Viv didn't believe me, but she nodded, smiled wide and long.

I chose the at-home option, because three to five minutes under anesthesia just didn't seem like enough suffering. The literature warned that some blood clots could be as big as lemons or oranges, and I couldn't help but think that fruit seemed a malicious analogy.

The painkillers did not help so much as abbreviate the wincing into smaller, simpler blocks. Despite precautions, the sheets were left stained; I disposed of them the next day and slept on the bare pilled mattress for nearly a month. I didn't tell anyone and simply stopped going to work, because the thought of nannying someone else's child seemed as impossible as time travel. The family left increasingly angry, then panicked voice mails. Sometimes I didn't hear the phone and sometimes I did, in which case I would watch it light up and vibrate with wonder. That the family I had worked for before—all things now categorized as before and after—still existed, still managed to force Brie and apple and candied walnut salads into their children's mouths before rushing out of their multimillion-dollar home, was hard to believe.

P aul forced his way in some six days or two weeks later and found me on the stained mattress watching television about the bottom of the ocean. I offered him something to drink and realized that all I had was long-expired soy milk (Jackson's) and a bottle of apple juice that had begun to ferment. I held it to the light and tilted it wistfully, watched it unsettle; it made me happy, in a small way, to see something change by my own hand, to observe another form rotting quietly.

When I returned, Paul was sitting on the bed—it felt wrong to see him sitting so casually on the physical space where I'd lost the last of Jackson and me—sorting through the pile of pamphlets and pill bottles I hadn't bothered to move.

"Jesus, Ida," he said. "Jesus Jesus Jesus." He looked down at where he sat, at the deep brown-and-red stain, and adjusted himself so that no part of his body touched it. He saw my face and froze.

"Sorry," he said. "It's just—"

• • •

I don't know how he managed to reach him, but he must have told Jackson, because shortly after the checks started coming; they bore no personal note, and absurd amounts of money. I called James, who confirmed that their grandfather, an oil-guy Texan they'd met twice who taught his dog to bark at the word "Democrat" and had never gotten along with his son and their father, had finally bit the old bullet and they'd both received enough money to last quite some time.

I t's too bad what I did to Paul. It's also too bad this is the best way I have of expressing it, and funny because I imagine that this is the way Jackson describes the way he treated me, artfully deflecting any blame: "It's too bad what happened with Ida." Too bad refers to that which was unavoidable in the wake of something greater or more important. It's too bad what I did to Paul, though in those months it grew to be a kind of playful diversion, testing the limits of manipulation possible through the arch of my back, the jut of my hipbones, a few words in the right places.

Paul clung even more heavily after the abortion and suggested in small ways how that particular expression of my vulnerability had begun to turn his feelings of friendship slowly into lust. He encouraged my every pathetic triumph and rewarded me with small tokens; whether I actively accepted them didn't matter. He was pleased when I showered, tousled my wet hair and complimented my scent;

he laughed loud and long when I made even the smallest, darkest joke; he praised the small herb garden on the fire escape (that I grew out of guilt for lying to James) and brought expensive fertilizers. It should also be said that he made his presence dependable when there were no small triumphs, when I began to revert to silence and starvation, and I began to rely on it. He was the only one who gave me permission. Instead of suffering alone, I let Paul come over and took pleasure in sending cruel words out of my mouth knowing there would be no consequences. Though I had, in a sense, grown to love them, these things I made, I forced him to watch while I hurled the potted plants off of the balcony and enjoyed his small moans.

He very nearly almost won. Somewhere in between the moments of the small triumphs and the fits, he nudged his way in. He made me smile. He showed up with Thai food and comforts and curiosities: an old cowboy belt buckle that concealed a fine silver lighter, sheets of luxuriously high thread counts, a bathrobe with deep pockets, etchings of various types of octopi.

And so, one night, while he happily supervised my consumption of too much whiskey and slowly placed his fingers on my back, I did not stiffen. And when he began kneading, it seemed, every single disk of my back into a singular and celebrated entity, I was grateful. And when he began to separate not just the muscles of my back but also my legs, I did not stop him. And when I couldn't hear the sounds of the film we'd been watching over his desperate grunting, I didn't complain, just kept staring and made up the characters' words, wrapped my legs around the small of his back halfheartedly, and observed as the two people on the screen exchanged proclamations of love and humor I wanted to understand but couldn't.

I am ashamed of the extravagant things I said and did in the weeks and months afterward, although I don't feel I had much choice given the way he grinned after we had sex, how he told me he loved me during. We took a vacation to Mexico that was in all regards perfect besides it being a lie, but he must have known on some level the fallacy of the sparkling lemonade we drank on those beaches, must have suspected the real reason I wanted him only on top with his head buried between my neck and shoulders. I loved Paul and still do, but could only stand it if I was able to memorize the ceiling above us. Our whole relationship, in retrospect, seems an exercise in ceilings; I praised him and lavished him in words of adoration and felt shocked at the levels of devotion he was willing to believe I felt sincerely.

In the Mexico photographs we look happy. There are several of him gesturing excitedly next to an eight-year-old who was drawing portraits on the street at the cost of one American dollar; Paul of course took a liking to him and bought six, one of me and one of him and one of us together, and three more of strangers who had decided against it after seeing the finished product. There's another in which I am holding up a margarita as large as my head and smiling so large my eyes and nose are overshadowed; another of me sleeping in the early morning, still wearing a cocktail dress from the night before, my hair falling off one side of the bed, nose perky, looking like someone you might like to cook breakfast for.

When we went to stay with my father, who needed supervision as Julia was visiting Jackson that weekend, I introduced Paul with no title. Paul assumed this was because I had already provided one in my biweekly telephone correspondence with my father, but in the living room he strained for recognition apologetically until finally he arrived at a beam and Paul returned it.

"Ah. Paul. I am *so* sorry. Our art dealer! Mr. Gallery. I've heard much about you, it's just, I'm afraid, with so much going in this ailing body of mine, I've gotten bad with details. It's such a relief to me, you being Ida's friend through all this heartache. It's hard for me and Julia, you know, being pretty much *both* of their parents . . ." and he trailed on, the sly smile of aging on his face.

"Friend?" Paul said to me on the drive home later, incredulously. "Friend?"

In the final ceiling Paul proposed in some sort of final threat, and I of course wept and told him I loved him but that I couldn't, and of course he begged, and of course I ran out of weeping probably too soon and it got too quiet, and of course he left, and of course we don't speak anymore.

While my magnetism to Jackson grew from an early age, it would be inaccurate to state he was the only magic. I loved James too—for being slightly younger and keeping me that way, for asking questions Jackson preferred not to, and later, for indulging in and nearly celebrating those unkempt aspects of his interior life.

Jackson considered; James evacuated then evaluated. As children, it was James who more actively encouraged that nonsensical landscape I remember and value. James who once fainted after individually bringing to life the eighty-five balloons he placed in his living room for no reason whatsoever except to surprise, then frustrate, then amuse his tired mother: it was hard to be actually mad at the playful air-filled globes, even if it made navigating through the space, after a twelve-hour day at a work, almost impossible. It was James who decided he would learn to juggle, and did, and insisted on teaching me though I was impatient and kept trying to give up, who clapped his hands and hollered in delight when I finally gave three oranges a place in the air. James who collected jokes and always had a new one to spare. Who remembered my mother's birthday and insisted we celebrate it every year. Who constructed the most elaborate forts that even Julia and my father would sneak in and wonder at: sometimes our respective living rooms remained in disarray for a full week, the couch cushions and tables all sacrificed for the sake of a home within a home, the specific and comforting brand of light that comes through a flannel sheet. James who enjoyed, once he was old enough for that kind of control, spelling my name or Jackson's in his urine, in immaculate cursive, all over town—who never stopped finding that hilarious. Eventually, I couldn't either. James who once taught a particularly malicious and buff foreign exchange student—who enjoyed calling certain vulnerable boys faggot and whispering terrible threats in their ears—a string of made-up words that the kid began using so frequently that he didn't make enough sense to be scared of anymore. On our own, James and I had a language, too. As children, we were best at concocting nonsense urgencies with mock terror, enjoyed breaking down the door of whichever available parent and crying: *It's Danny! Down at the old hotel with the hose again!* never maintaining our composure for very long. And later, once words had grown from toys to tools to toys again, inventing idioms without breaking stride. *You know what they say*, James would begin, *You don't go crying into your soup and expect a steak. True,* I would say. *And likewise, there's a good reason not to trust a sparrow in a gold mine.*

James whose sweetness, if frantic, was almost always evident. Who always asked me, in the morning, what my dreams were like. Who gently prodded at my quiet, when it constructed in a dark way, suggested that we explore it.

Just after the deterioration of Paul and me, and just before James's terrifying walks, he appeared in my doorway and we began sleeping together. It should be said that we remained fully clothed and never returned to the naked state we'd so many times shared in the bathtub as children, although I can't assert that the level of intimacy did not reach levels that felt like betrayal to Jackson, whom I still felt I belonged to.

We were comparable to magnets. No choice but to join. Both with minds whirring darkly and constantly, both hoping the noise of the other might drown out our interiors. Mostly we slept. Sometimes I sobbed and James looked at me with a curiosity that was uncomfortably reminiscent of Jackson. Once we bought two boxes of the most expensive donuts our city had to offer and egged each other on to keep eating until we ran to the bathroom and vomited, our cheeks pressed against the other's and our bile merging. I took up residence at his house, returning once a week or less if I could help it to the apartment that smelled less like Jackson and more like abandonment every day; I hurried in holding my breath and exchanged clothing for other clothing, as if I had anyone to impress who might notice I'd been wearing the same oversized sweater. Once, in a gesture I felt proud of for days on end, I opened all the windows and left them like that, as if to say: *Let something fly in. Anything.*

We ordered in and bought microwave dinners by the dozen. We let the garbage overflow onto the floor, a magnificent display of color and texture and smell, and took pride in how little we interacted with the outside world. We bought a sixty-pack of crayons and a two hundred-pack of paper and felt proud for coating the leaflets with such thick layers of wax.

Despite having enough money to completely retreat into his troubled brain, James kept his job at the hotel, though complaints from customers grew more frequent and his manager gently suggested he think about taking a serious vacation. While he was at work I stayed in his apartment, watching a million of channels of cable. I cried when Thelma and Louise went off that cliff and thought about what I'd heard once at a party, that the filmmakers had nearly released the film with an alternate ending in which the car hits the ground and keeps going. I watched reality television shows about people with drug problems and felt envious of their families and friends who crowded around them in a gaggle of support and love and forgiveness. I drooled and breathed deeply while on

the stand-up comedy channel black people talked about
white people and white people talked about how it wasn't
okay to talk about black people. More often than not I
fell asleep to lugubrious documentaries about the forgotten industrial wasteland of Middle America or black-
and-white Hitchcocks; in my dreams I wandered through
abandoned sewing factories or sat in the lush train cars of
the 1940s, trying to remember my destination or realizing,
when the conductor came by to collect tickets, that I had
released mine out the window and watched it skirt the
Midwestern winds. On good nights James would come
back from the graveyard shift, turn the television off, and
crawl into bed, adjusting his body to fit with mine; if I
woke he would kiss the tip of my nose and whisper "How
many?" as in "How many brain cells did you kill watching all that television?" and I would reply "So many I
have lost the ability to count," and draw him closer. On
bad nights he didn't get into bed at all. I would wake and
find him on the tiny back patio, relating to a full ashtray,
shivering and not wanting to talk or talking about things
I couldn't understand. I would coax him inside, take off
his shoes, move his stiff joints so that I could remove his
jacket, hand him the remote. The images from the still-
on television reflected in his eyes, and he let them play
there.

I left after three weeks, feeling, for the first time in so
long, awake, and conscious of the fact I had done what
Jackson had always wanted: I had slept and slept and slept.
On my way to the door I stopped at the kitchen table, where

James sat coloring, his beard overgrown and unkempt. I offered to take out the garbage but he shrugged and didn't look up, and I understood that this was what James's life was like, that my being there had prompted nothing. As much as I didn't want it to be the case, what I had was different from what he did.

James has always been, by definition and religion, a walker; he has always used it as a freedom, an essential mental space to visit frequently. So when he began dissociating—the term we were taught later to use that referred to a tendency to lose all sense of his surroundings—it was initially difficult to recognize it as such. He had showed up at my apartment just before I followed him back to his and ended up staying. While he had the address but had never visited, while he told me he didn't quite know how he had gotten there, it didn't strike me as strange. I didn't realize that he'd literally begun floating in and out of awareness, that he would look up and find he'd traveled miles without any memory of the trip. I told him I wasn't sure how I'd gotten here either and invited him in without a second thought.

Following the suicide attempt that resulted in hospitalization and the initial diagnosis of bipolar disorder, it seemed

James learned pretty quickly and effortlessly how to avoid repeats, claiming he couldn't afford to take off any more time at work. He was, is, a fascinating creature, and he had made a practice of using it to his advantage in social situations, not excluding psychiatry and therapy. During a brief experiment with group therapy he proved himself the most popular among the crumbling circle—the others found themselves identifying with his feedback the most, even sometimes asking the therapist to let him go on speaking after she'd identified a good "building point" or whatever and cleared her throat to begin.

Before Jackson left and prior to the onset of James's new and disturbing type of walks, his therapist requested he bring in a family member, and he chose me. Given that he and his brother had barely spoken since the hospital, the both of them too uncomfortable with the parallel loss of control in their lives, the both of them insisting they were worse off, I agreed. It became clear almost instantly that this was meant to be some sick sort of in-joke between the two of us, him using every psychological cliché in the book and seeming desperate for the woman's approval, her discussing with me the ways in which James had grown since their first visit.

I don't know for certain that there were other attempts, though I do know that there were several occasions when I called the hotel on nights he always worked and some hoarse-throated older woman or squeaky-voiced kid answered and told me he wasn't working. James never called in sick to work, and so this meant he was pained in a worse way.

On one of these occasions, hoarse-throated Patty asked
who might be calling, please, and I said Ida, and she clucked
her tongue.

"Oh, Ida, honey," she said. "I am just so sorry. Know
that I'm praying for you and James both," and I rushed off
the phone in a panic to call my father and affirm whichever
awful truth.

My father picked up with a cheery clearing of the throat
and a singsong "I was just thinking of you." When I asked
how he was, he said that everything was quite good; autumn had always been his favorite time of year, Julia'd tried
her hand at mulled wine and they'd indulged heavily the
night before (much background laughter on her part at this
one), and his lungs had actually been feeling better than
they had in months!

I never called out James on his lie, knowing he must have
been off on a pretty terrible vacation to tell it. I called his
landline—he has never and probably will never have a cell
phone—about six times, with increasing frequency, but I
never reached him and for some reason I just believed and
hoped he was all right and just out on a walk instead of taking the bus over there or calling my father and Julia back to
fill them in. It's ridiculous the way all three of us retained
that childhood bond of keeping secrets from the adults no
matter the cost, insisted on naming it us versus them when
it had become so clearly us versus us, when we as a unit had
ceased to function in any benefit to each other and instead
just rolled around like marbles waiting to be arranged.

The scary-long walks as opposed to the standard: they were a strong indicator that the just plain sad, which landed James once in the hospital and then in pretty regular therapy and an antidepressant haze, had mutated into something else. In the same us-versus-them philosophy we used with Julia and my father, I didn't tell James's therapist about the phone call in which he revealed his little project of writing eulogies for the living. Neither did I tell his therapist or our parents about the other increasingly terrifying phone calls and incidents. Sadness is one thing, insanity another, and the second I've so romanticized and linked with many other things (like *beauty* and *art* and *love*) that it was hard isolating it from the rest, holding it up to the fluorescent and brutally honest lighting it required.

He told me, at one point, that he was considering getting rid of his books. When I asked why, he told me nonplussed that he was holding a new belief that with so many old stories around, no other stories could be created. This was poetic up until he told me how long "it has been Tuesday." He was convinced the books were linked to time, if only his conception of it; he mentioned that naturally *his* time was different from mine. Something sick had made a home in his head, and it had named itself after a day of the week and lent itself to his obsession.

I got off the phone and repeated his words in my head. Things become understandable with familiarity, and so I thought: *It has been Tuesday for so long. It has been Tuesday for so long. It has been Tuesday for so long.* I wanted to discern, but couldn't, and it was then I admitted that James's own personal Tuesday cage was something much beyond poetics or standard feelings of emptiness and worthlessness.

Despite my omissions, despite James's talents for manipulation, he ultimately garnered a new diagnosis. "Borderline personality disorder" is a term that scares most people, but for all of us it was a relief, a label, a home. It framed his love affair with speed and called that compulsive behavior, named that haunting distinction he had held over time and Tuesdays an inflated sense of self. James finally had the license he'd been driving without illegally for so long— or rather, walking. We learned this after his walks became increasingly scary, and more than once did I have to take a cab to a strange neighborhood where he had somehow managed to find one of probably seven remaining pay phones in the city. Finally one evening, unable to see any beauty in his lost, incapable of branding it special, I called Julia and my father.

He lives at their house now and is mostly happy, his whims indulged, all the time to write songs he can manage and a ration of two beers a day (against doctor's orders but my father insisted the man be allowed his hops). He is frustrated by not being able to go more than a couple blocks alone, but it being our hometown he pretty intelligently realizes he knows it all intimately and so is content to bake with Julia or just eat her baking, excel at the crossword puzzle and put it on the fridge, watch a marathon of *The Twilight Zone*.

Airports and airplanes, to me, still seem like the happy future we've all been told so much about. So many small pleasures exist in hurtling toward the ones we miss: the cheerful assistance of the steel moving walkway, the ready availability of anything we might need in miniature or in excess, the series of immaculate and anonymous spaces. Today is dark and I should not find joy in so many colors of toothbrushes, their frills reduced to syllogism— you will find no tongue scraper on this product, sir, only reds and blues and simple utility—but I can't help it.

Today is dark and I should not take pleasure in the toilets that flush so promptly and politely, but I cannot help but find them kind and I thank them silently for removing the evidence I was there. I may be losing my mind.

I am hurtling toward what, today? What will I answer if a kind old woman happens to sit next to me in seat 17C (aisle)? Am I allowed to simply state, "Going to see my father"? And why should I feel guilty for not revealing the very whole truth to a woman I don't know and will never see again? Why should I let my time in the air be about a funeral? I have paid several hundred dollars for the clear space, the small oval window, the seat designed to recline farther than ever, the odd-sized can of Coca-Cola, and I intend to enjoy them anyway I please.

I *am* going to see my father today, though he promises to look very much different and remain silent. That ghostliness aside, today I am also hurtling toward Jackson; I will see him for the first time in two years, four months, and sixteen days. When he began calling so casually seven months ago, just after I finally exited the city we'd called ours, I never once said: Please explain yourself. Please help me to understand what you did to me, what I did to you, what we did to each other. Instead I rose to the occasion of witty banter, and when he mentioned her I covered the mouthpiece so he would not hear the gnarled cough-sob that escaped without my permission. I was esoteric and clever and not actively kind, and made every effort to receive his phone calls but not dial his number and generally achieved the flippancy he had provided as the tone of our telephone interactions.

Oh-ha-ha, how very funny it all was—that the problem *had* ceased since us but he was pretending it hadn't in order to save his ass. What a terrible person I am, he mused, and I laughed with him as if I hadn't been directly ravaged by his terribleness. It was my fault just as much as his: I gave him permission to walk right back into the us versus them we'd spent so many years practicing.

I let him drop her name, her boring Midwestern name with its bland consonance, and said nothing when he went on about her virtues, how he didn't quite appreciate them as much as he should, but was trying; how he knew blaming it on the sleepwalking was immoral but felt she'd be more hurt if she knew the full truth; how he just didn't think she could handle that sort of pain and so it felt like the only option. And I didn't need to say—then why not leave her? He answered that, too, as if I had asked: "She's the sort of person I *should* love, I, and I think I will if I work at it."

I had plotted the joining of our new adult-sized bodies carefully, certain that an event so many years in the making demanded forethought and atmospheric perfection. The afternoon preceding it, fifteen-year-old Jackson sat on my toilet while I cut my hair, bits of his face showing up in the mirror with the movement of my hands and elbows, his lips in the glass image positioned just so in the curvature of my armpit. The bathtub, once a container for our naked bodies and more innocent mischief, reflected also. Did he receive the glances I designed as seductive bouncing toward him? Did he understand that the thin black cotton of my shirt intentionally highlighted my chest? Did he have any idea?

I pushed the broom with efficiency and gestured for him to follow me. My mother's long-weary bag, patched and repatched for over a decade, already packed with the supplies I'd deemed necessary. We took our normal route downtown, through the streets where our peers sat on benches waiting for their lives to start, down the cobbled alley that ran along the west side of the river, past the same waterside café where our parents had jiggled us on their laps and first begun to realize the full weight of adulthood. On the backside of the long-obsolete mill, which became a home to women's clothing stores and wine bars and shops that sold rocks and candles, we climbed a set of steps to get to a balcony we frequented. From there, one could look down on the water and see it almost as innocent as the tourists did, feel a civic pride.

A few weeks before, I'd discovered a series of beams and pipes at the landing of the stairs. With a few shifts of weight they served as a ladder to a ledge onto the roof. The top of the mill was like an uninhabited city; it sloped in on itself and rose up again in tens of different places. Much of it was the corrugated steel of the exterior that was visible to passersby below, and other parts were gravel-covered concrete. It spanned almost two blocks. I'd begun escaping up there and eventually assembling a landscape with which to surprise Jackson. In a rectangular area lower than the rest, with four walls and the sky overhead, I'd placed sunflowers in pots around the perimeter, spread a quilt in the center.

He smiled when he saw it, threw his arms skyward in surrender. He'd lived alongside my elaborate plots long enough, seen them both fail and flourish. This one, surely, a success we could settle into for the afternoon. Feeling freed by the scenery, as I hoped he would, Jackson settled his head into my lap and I dared to stroke his hair behind his ears. Growing bolder, I asked him to sit, brought out the pint of whiskey and pulled on it and passed him the bottle. I started coughing, and so did he, and we slapped each other on the back until the coughing had ceased and we started to laugh. We passed the bottle back and forth in silence, both feeling a little sick. We talked about my father, about his mother, about people we found boring, the whole time trying to catch glances of the other like we so often do while passing by windows and wanting to get a look at ourselves. With the end of the bottle, my heart felt rich, and we were confusing syllables more often than not.

He cleared his throat in a serious manner, and I worried he suspected me, that he'd subvert my intentions before even exploring them.

"I have to tell you something," he whispered.

"You have a very pretty hair and mouth"—I took his hand—"and also . . . I like boobs. I mean your boobs. I mean I like lots of boobs but I mean I think your brets are beautiful. Breasts."

It felt like the moment at which you stand waist deep in the water, preparing your body for full submersion. Trying to feel what it means to be underwater beforehand, that release, though imagining it proves impossible.

"I have to tell you something too," I managed through the weight of my tongue.

"Shoot," he said, formed a gun out of his fingers and pointed it at the sky, then made a little *ka-bloom* sound and blew at the smoking gun but miscalculated and ended up spitting all over one of his knuckles.

We laughed, falling into each other and redoing the big gun joke like can you believe how funny we are? And then redoing the gun joke again and laughing some more. When the explosions settled, we found ourselves with my legs around his waist. I crafted a pistol out of his left hand and my right one, and pointed the tip up at the sky.

Things I remember: the green-blue wrapper of the condom, the awkwardness of teeth in too-eager mouths, the seeming multiplication of limbs, the bits of gravel that made their way onto the blanket. That once he made his way in we gaped at how easy it really was to bind two people together. That when it came it almost hurt, that my hands spread out taut and joyous like starfish on his back, that it was warm and sweet and I wanted to make shelter within it.

When James called to tell me my father died, he told me he planned to take over his garden.

"Basil and thyme and I don't know maybe even an avocado tree or peaches I have heard are not always that hard if you're . . . and tomatoes and anything you want, I, and you'll always come for dinner and I'll cook for you and it will be so delicious you'll cry, I, because he's not there to taste it, yeah, but mostly because he would have been so proud and . . ."

And he went on and on, and his mania was so generous it felt like an assimilation of gentle, and I felt like he was right next to me kissing my forehead too insistently, and I remembered that there's not just one who calls me I. There are three of us.

My father retained such intellectual strength that over the phone it was often easy to forget the physical weakening, turn an ear away during the gasping pauses, but it was more and more impossible to paint it all brightly when Jackson and I, still a unit, visited him. It rattled Jackson more than it did me, probably because he'd chosen to love my father whereas I had since before I possessed the words to describe the loveliness that was hiding in his neck, safe in his narrative. He didn't like seeing him bound mostly to his chair, would start biting the half-moons from his fingernails the moment my father started discussing the latest reports from the doctor. As if to thwart the topic's mention, he always arrived so lively, so well-read, so full of other things to speak of. My father grinned at the interruptions, though when Jackson turned to Julia to overflow his charisma onto her, he would clasp my hand and twinkle at me in the slow the way the dying do, and I would nod. We were both more worried for Jackson than we were for ourselves.

Jackson and I began spending more and more weekends there with the fading of his health, though Jackson claimed it only a reprieve from the city, while I felt more at home under the pressing weight of my father's disease. A newspaperman his whole life: this was just one more deadline, one more story going to press, and I liked to think of the moment he stopped typing and stood up and pushed his chair in with precision; of the way he would insist, after, on a drive; of the release he always felt, postpublishing; of his byline, the printed letters that formed his name behind the plastic of the newspaper box. Throughout my childhood, I would put a quarter in the slot, watch the frozen president disappear, slowly turn the steel latch, and reach into the dark space to bring my father into the light.

One Saturday at my father's house, I woke to find my childhood bed still smelling but absent of Jackson. Julia, just waking with coffee in the kitchen, hadn't seen him, and we set about calling his phone repeatedly, assuming the worst. His car—ours—was gone, and we hoped against hope his sleep hadn't discovered how to move Park to Drive. When he never answered she grabbed her large key ring and we rolled through the downtown, only finding a new generation of young mothers, teenage café employees flipping signs to open, joggers intent on their journey. Back at home, we opted not to tell my father, distracting him instead with the newspaper, fresh-squeezed orange juice. At ten o'clock Jackson appeared, the look on his face the holiness that occurs after a long time alone, and told us to get in the car.

It was stunning to see him an administrator, to watch him wrap the blue silk tie around my father's field of vision, grinning. Julia, who knew and spoke with the deterioration of my father's health every day, cast nervous glances and fiddled with the radio and asked my father how he was doing back there one too many times. I held his fingers in mine, his portable oxygen tank between my knees as we curved up through the California hills, happy, for once, to yield, to be a passenger. When Jackson finally slowed to a halt on the uneven dirt shoulder, unbuckled the strap across his shoulder, Julia turned to me with such a panicked look that I reached for her hand and told her it would be okay.

"What will be okay," my father asked. "What?"

"Mom," Jackson asserted. "Please." The first word confident, the second desperate.

He helped my father out of the car, put an arm around his waist, and gestured for me to do the same. We made our way down the incline, my father quiet though clearly petrified, his body unwilling to do the things it had loved so.

"Three points of contact," I offered, then repeated, and he nodded and breathed the way they'd taught him, no matter that the exercises were meant to get him through a day at home, maybe around the block, and never down the untended earth.

It was spectacular and whole and remains an image that feeds me. The reclining padded chair placed just so in the shallow edge of the clear river, a parasol worked into its crown. Just next to it, a tall metal table positioned in the stones, on it resting volumes of my father's favorite writers, a single proud sunflower, a pen and paper, a cooler full of fruits and drinks and sweet things. Jackson returned my father's sight once we emerged from the path onto the little beach, and his already struggling lungs just couldn't cope, and he had to sit immediately and rest awhile before we escorted him to this throne. He barely touched the books that day, sampled only briefly the cherries, just sat there with his feet up and sipped the bitter favorite beer he rarely indulged in anymore. Across the river Jackson kept disappearing and reappearing on various points of the rocks that faced us, sprouting triumphantly like the unlikely green jutting out in strange angles, and my father yelled and cheered every time he leaped into the water, urging him to jump from higher and higher points and clasping the fingers of Julia, who hovered nearby, trying to find her home in the water.

Julia had prepared fanatically, as if trying to impress him or finally say yes, yes, I loved you, love you, will keep loving you.

When I arrived, James, in his mother's apron, was on a manic upswing, chopping vegetables into fine and finer pieces in the kitchen, carrying snack plates back and forth from the kitchen, asking how I was but lacking the attention span to listen. He was twisting his hair like he used to, and a spray of half-smoked cigarettes kept accumulating on the front porch—he felt, I think, too guilty to smoke the whole thing, knowing this was the pleasure my father had lived and died for.

Photos of my father were everywhere; I could tell Julia wished they always had been, and as such had framed some of them and tried to place others in locations where people put photographs of those still alive: on the refrigerator at a jaunty angle, amid others on the couch-side table in the living room, on her bureau.

I found myself sneering. Hadn't she been ready? This was obviously an expression of my own guilt for not admitting that his struggle really was reaching its end point. I replayed the last time we spoke on the telephone and attempted to gain some final piece of paternal wisdom. What had he said? And I? And how long did we pause between sentences? And did we laugh?

I tried to tell myself it was a shame, an unfortunate coincidence and nothing more, that the last dialogue I'd had with my father had lacked his general stubborn cheer. He hadn't even feigned with the "There was something I wanted to tell you but have forgotten." He came to me as an old man who wanted to talk and me to listen.

There was none of his softness. He cleared his throat and wheezed and began to tell me about the night before my mother died. "There's no other way to put it, Ida. I had too much to drink. Had too much goddamn liquor. I'd been home all week with you—Mollie was out looking for a job and shopping for goddamn new paint samples for the kitchen even though we'd just—goddamn it we'd just *painted* the kitchen—and getting coffee with all these new women who went to private colleges in Vermont and had kids around your age—and finally I said, look, I've been here in this house all week and I need out"—he was talking too fast and stopped to catch his breath in big gulps, which was exactly what the exercises recommend he not do—"and she said okay fine, you're right. Okay.

"So we got Julia to come over—her and your mom liked each other all right, actually—did you know the boys were with you the last night your mom was alive? And anyway, Ida, we went down to the Central Club on my insisting. I said, honey, I want a real bar with pool tables and cheap drinks, and your mother said yes even though she didn't like the idea. That place was pretty bad then, worse than now if you can believe it, and pretty soon after we sat down it was a scary scene. Every guy in the place was staring at her—she was way too pretty, way too smart—and she didn't like it. I tried to take her mind off of it, suggested we play a game of pool, but your mother . . . when she was mad like that, she couldn't focus. She shot a terrible game and the whole time these assholes were starting to snicker, but your mother . . . she had always refused to let me treat her like a lady, do you understand? 'None of that Southern charm shit,' she always said, always pushed the door open for herself, rarely even let me"—he gasped here but in a different way, the kind that precedes a great opening up of the body for a sob—"never even let me coddle her. Ida, are you listening?"

(I was listening, was transfixed. I was also considering what else I had inherited from my father: that insistence that the audience *look* and *listen*. How many times had I pleaded to Jackson: *Look. Listen. Are you listening? Do you understand?* But not stopped to hear his reply. My father didn't stop either.)

"And so I kept tough on her, didn't give her any breaks. Pretty much all her balls were on the table and I had three left. She told me she was leaving and I said, hey, come on. Don't be a poor sport. But she left, Ida, and I didn't follow her—if I had tried to she wouldn't have let me, do you understand? And so I stayed, had a grand old time feeling like I was, you know, 'integrating with the locals.' Some idiot was impressed by my being a newspaperman, the stories I told him, and he gave me, I kid you not, a hat and a steak. He was a meat delivery guy and his truck was out back, went out there and got me a steak and gave me the hat off his head. Don't know why about the hat, still."

My father laughed, here, and it was the closest to the hoot he once famously produced I'd heard in a couple of years, until he remembered what story he was telling, exactly.

"But Ida I stayed 'til last call. I don't really remember the walk home, quite, but I know I had the mind to put that steak in the freezer and crawl into bed. And that's it. I remember vaguely that I was looking forward to telling your mother about this guy, about him insisting I take his meat and the hat, that I knew she would laugh at what an asshole she'd been to leave and what an asshole I'd been to stay and get so tossed. I remember planning on a big dinner for the three of us the next night—even though your teeth weren't ready yet, I remember thinking, yeah, baby's first steak, and smiling at the future memory.

"Only, Ida, I didn't hear her. I was sleeping off the cheap whiskey the steak guy bought me and I didn't wake. The only time in her life your mother actually needed me, actually called out for me, and I didn't hear her."

I was touched that my father had come to me and not Julia. Touched that he saw me stable enough to take this, digest it, and still love him; touched he was still able to laugh about the hat and the steak; touched by how clearly I was a combination of the both of them; touched by being a part of a real live, honest-to-goodness family made of bloodlines and shared genetics who did not up and go whenever they felt like it except when death gave them no choice. When I went to respond, though, my father stopped me.

"Dear heart," he gasped, "I shouldn't . . . I shouldn't have talked like that so long. Gets my blood pressure high and my heart sad. Tired, now. I've got to get off the phone, okay?"

He sounded panicked. I wanted to tell him I loved him and ask where Julia was, whether he was all right, but he was already gone. I almost called back several times that night, but part of the deal between us was that mostly we pretended the other was fine—it helped us believe it to be true about ourselves.

I was replaying this conversation for perhaps the twenty-second time that day when Jackson arrived. He was dressed far too well in clothing I'd never seen before, and it pained me to think of him in that dressing room across the country, turning his cheek under the flattering lights, strolling out to show Shannon the precision of the wool slacks and the softness of the sweater. We locked eyes and I was the first to break and turn, but he crossed the room and wrapped his arms around me, and I let him. I remained in the pocket between his shoulder and chest too long, taking pleasure in the fact that his scent had not changed.

There were still three hours before the Ceremony of Life Julia had planned. Jackson suggested a walk and I obliged, seeing as Julia's buzz was pretty thoroughly terrifying and evidence of my father was everywhere. We walked past the park where we had smoked pot for the first time together, in the rain under the shelter of a slide long gone and replaced with one of bright plastics; cut through the playground and kicked the sand in defiance. It was bright and ninety degrees and the moments rippled into the next unnaturally. Sensing my discomfort, Jackson pulled out a pair of sunglasses and placed them on my face, and under their costume my eyes became oceans. We didn't speak as we crossed by the picnic tables, although Jackson did stoop to see whether the words he'd engraved with his knife remained on the underside of one of them, and though he didn't tell me what he was looking for I knew what it meant when he nodded with satisfaction.

Like always, we were headed for the river. It smelled especially strong in the heat, and we walked the lengths of the docks sneering at the tourists, who were out on the decks of their yachts on chairs of stretched pale pink linen and cherrywood. My father had always joked about buying a shitty boat to park next to theirs, naming it *Privilege* and barbecuing discount chicken wings and publicly drinking the cheapest beer available all day long and being just unyieldingly friendly to all of them.

Instead of talking about my father, though, Jackson and I talked about him. About how he started having sex with other people and not coming home to Shannon and telling her the sleepwalking had started again and he didn't know where he'd been those times she woke up to find him gone. About how she'd been unbelievably forgiving and sympathetic and offered to give up sleep to watch over him or maybe find them a house in the country and invest in very complicated locks. About how she had listened and nodded while he talked about me and asked questions and tried to believe his reflections on our disintegration were healthy, even integral. About how when he started pushing it and even going so far as to steal Shannon's car in the middle of the night and fuck this bartender with a long black braid in the backseat and purposefully come all over the upholstery and feign complete wonderment, Shannon just, well, took it, and started buying literature about sleep disorders and highlighting the texts in neat, cheerfully colored lines and joining online discussion groups. About how finally he slept with one of her best friends, a blonde with decent breasts but a slight limp from some growth disorder or another, and while following this instance he offered no apologies or excuses or displacement of blame, Shannon even tried for a little while to convince herself and him that he had slept through it. And so when he got the news about William, he said, that seemed like a pretty good reason to pack up and return to the familiar part of the country.

Ida, he said, upon waking from his story, I miss you. And I couldn't say anything, because he'd offered the words I'd needed for so long, only now they seemed hollow and extra, now they floated in front of us with neither a home nor a future.

When I had implied I was maybe too weak to plan the whole thing, Julia offered wholeheartedly to undertake the task, and I agreed. She consulted me, of course—which kind of flowers, how did I feel about having the ceremony on a boat, was there anything else I wanted to include—and I replied in short answers, stressing only that I wanted all the guests dressed formally, as if for a grand party. She made a little noise with her throat and began to point out something or other but gave up, and I told her, for the first time, that I loved her. She released a warble *coo* and emphasized that she loved me as well, and I thought of her decades ago framed by the sunlight in their kitchen with the phone cord wrapped around and around her fingers, her morning hair still gnarled in the back where she'd slept on it and her wrapping her robe tighter and tighter around herself and rejoicing in new and tiny folds of warmth. About how she had run away to Mexico, once James and Jackson were grown, bought a surplus of bright-colored dresses and went dancing, realized that was all she had needed, really, and come back to Madrone Street and moved in with my father.

Julia must have read somewhere about the flowers and the baguettes; it was too bizarre an idea (especially given the context) on its own. She asked James and Jackson to poke the holes with a large serrated knife and invited me to put the bouquets inside them. The wind from the bay bit the back of my neck and I shrugged and trusted her, though in truth the whole loaves of sourdough bread made my mouth water and I wanted to fill myself with them instead of their sliced counterpart on the slightly swaying snack table. It was supposed to be the opening event, us his official and unofficial children placing the bread in the water. But the flowers didn't stay upright, and the waves beneath tugged at the stems and deconstructed the bouquetlike quality above, and everyone in attendance stopped watching and thumbed the memorial pamphlet once again or excused themselves to the small bathroom beneath the deck, where the smells of cleaning products and years of brine played equal parts and the toilet roared when it flushed.

Here my memory fails me. I know I was handed the ashes and I know I looked to James and Jackson and they both nodded encouragingly. I know I strangely felt the need for proper etiquette and looked out at everyone and thanked them for coming. I know I expected something much finer and winced at the coarseness and the clumps of what must have been bone; I know that James and Jackson each put a hand on my shoulder blade for each parent I was now without; I know that on the drive home I insisted we stop for the authentic saltwater taffy that tourists pay top dollar for and Julia falsified enthusiasm; I know I stuffed my face with the ocean until I was so thirsty I couldn't imagine a time I hadn't been and remembered something my father used to say with a mirthful twist of his lips when a lightbulb when out: "It is until it isn't."

I asked to sleep in his room. Julia kept insisting that if I even slightly did not feel up to going through my father's things that she would of course keep them safe. It was un-spoken, but Julia wanted to go on fingering his neatly hung sweaters and alphabetized books, imagining the names of people in boxes of photographs she'd never seen before, and so when I said that yes, I might like to wait, she beamed and squeezed my shoulder. And so I resolved to leave all the proof for future perusal, mine the memories later. I found myself more interested in the utilitarian or recent objects he'd left behind, anyway: the razor that still held his hair, the keys he had turned in the sticky lock not four days ago, the Post-it he had placed on his bedroom mirror that read, inexplicably: AND WHERE WERE THE ALLIGATORS?! a private joke with himself I would never understand.

I sat on his carefully made bed, feeling the firmness my father had slept on, looked at the ceiling he'd memorized with years of insomnia. On his bedside table was his wal-let, the same he'd used for years. I found his most recent video store receipt, noted how well-worn his library card, removed the store of photos from their bulging plastic envelopes. My mother covered in yellow paint in our kitchen, grinning and holding the roller as if it was a trophy; Jackson and me as toddlers naked in a bathtub with bubble beards; his mother and father in 1940s church attire; James and his Godzilla in our front yard, looking ominous and not interested in the camera; every school photograph I'd ever taken. Hidden away in the folds were even more pictures: friends dead for decades, a face I recognized as a Frenchwoman he'd had a torturous affair with by the name on the back. I looked at every business card and unfolded every piece of paper. One, a scrap of a legal pad that I took at first for another private reference or corner of his brain, featured a bullet list with accompanying value symbols, names, and email addresses, and I understood quickly that these were the identities of the people who'd bid on Jackson's work. I returned everything else hastily and entered the living room, where James was sleeping with Jackson on the small futon. I nearly woke them to share my discovery, but instead I got in between their bodies and waited, stiffly, to understand what had changed with the departure of my father. As if feeling my warmth through their dreams, they made small adjustments, turned to me in increments that were small until they weren't—*it isn't until it is*—until both had draped their limbs around mine so intricately that I couldn't move if I tried and I fought off sleep vehemently, determined to appreciate what they gave me without my even asking.

ACKNOWLEDGMENTS

I must first give thanks to the memory of my father, a writer who always encouraged me to find the right words. I wish to also acknowledge professors Logan Esdale and James Blaylock of Chapman University, for giving light and time to the tiniest saplings of this; my mother, for carrying laughter and wisdom in her purse, and Ben Marsh, for sharing the weight; James Pittmann, for gifting me an escape and an anonymous space in which to write; the community of Fayetteville, Arkansas, for receiving me with such kindness; Brent Hoff, for helping these characters find their way home; my agent, Victoria Marini, for finding me and fighting for me; Jerry Delacruz, champion of the late-night heart-to-heart; my editor, Corinna Barsan, for breathing grace onto these pages; Isaac Fitzgerald, an unyielding cheerleader from the first; Olivia Harrison, a reliable source of laughter and love since preschool; Lucius Bono, who came to the rescue more times than I can count and composed missives that fed me; Jessica Brownell, for adopting me and holding my hand; Gabriel Magaña, the kindest of cowboys; my sister, Vanessa Penn, whose dance upon my life is immeasurable; the town of Petaluma, a place impossible to forget; and the city of San Francisco, which generously lends itself to stories.

ABOUT THE AUTHOR

Born and raised in northern California, Kathleen Alcott studied in southern California, lived in San Francisco, and presently resides in Brooklyn, New York. Her work has appeared in *American Short Fiction*; *Slice*; *Explosion-Proof*; The Rumpus.net; *Rumpus Women, Volume 1*, an anthology of personal essays; and elsewhere. She is currently at work on her second novel, a work that traces the lives of four tenants of an apartment building in New York City.